Watch Over Me:
A Witch's Tale

Ajay Bell

ISBN (Hardcover): 979-8-9985652-0-5
ISBN (Paperback): 979-8-9985652-1-2

Contents

Preface

The 1600s. A time of crisis, hysteria, and chaos that disrupted the puritan way of life in colonial America. Witch trials have spilled over from England, leading to some of the largest convictions and slaughters in America's history. Often presumed guilty until proven innocent, thousands of individuals have lost their lives to witchcraft accusations and word-of-mouth, all backed with minimal reputable evidence. While legal notes and documents have been maintained with fine detail and accuracy, the perspective of the accused is often left unnoted. The sheer torture, hardship, fear, and tragic endings for these victims must be understood and recognized.

I

Warren Hollow

Autumn's chill is upon us. Farming season rests as we prepare our crops for the long harvest ahead. Each day lingers shorter than the last, with night growing more prevalent in the evening hours. Wind blows with an intensifying sharpness as the sting of winter makes its presence known. Falling leaves and decaying vegetation indicate a deferment to farming for the lasting winter. 'Twas a difficult winter for our village of Warren Hollow last year, as long months of heavy snowfall prolonged the return of cultivation. The rapidly changing weather indicates that this winter shall be no better.

Although a time of uncertainty is near, I undoubtedly favor autumn for boundless reasons. Nature has always spoken to me and speaks the loudest through the aura of fall. When chores have ended and my presence has no requirement at home, I often spend the days exploring the forest for hours on end. In the present, I am returning in reluctance to our village from yet another magnificent forest venture. I've made my way through the back gate, following the trail and waving to those who pass by and offer greetings from their homes. Suddenly, I am startled by the commotion of a nearby family in distress and halt my steps. A young child draws my attention. He is likely my brother's age or younger and holds a pumpkin that displays a poorly carved expression on the front.

"We must dispose of such wickedness at once," his mother exclaims, "thou knowest All Hallows Eve be a day of evil and corruption!"

She rips the pumpkin from her child's hands and continues to scold his behavior. In her state of fury, the woman notices my gaze, hastily rushing her child inside out of fear and embarrassment.

If only I could tell her to fear not, I also hold a love for the mystery and frolic surrounding All Hallows Eve. All children in Warren Hollow share the same notion, from the youngest to the oldest of us.

Celebrations in such a manner are unthinkable in our village, or anywhere within the Massachusetts colony in truth, as convictions surrounding satanism and witchcraft have begun to tear through our entire way of life. We exist in a time of crisis and hysteria, with executions now resulting from abrupt witch hunts. Families spend fortnights engaged in prayer at the church, begging for God's forgiveness and trying to gain knowledge on something none of us understand. Some children have claimed affliction from witchcraft, spreading rumors and strange accusations under the pressure of the Reverend or our parents. In turn, the rest of us children have halted our regular bonfire excursions in the forest for fear of conviction.

Will witchcraft plague my family someday? How could it, we are pure and dedicated to our prayer and faith? What would Mother and Father say if they discovered that I have been taking my younger brother to the forest bonfires with the other children of the village?

Constant thoughts crowd my focus as I arrive back to our property. I notice Mother is bound in a concerning discussion with Father regarding my brother, John, and the apothecary.

"We must stand by our dear friend Rose," Mother states in panic, "I fear that she will hang if someone does not rise in support. Rose has saved John's life so somebody must save hers. Maybe we could talk to Reverend Thomas and -"

"Silence!" Father shouts as irritation and concern boils within him, "if we continue speaking of such actions then we too shall be labeled as heathens!"

John was born into an unfortunate existence of illness and ailment. Mother and Father did everything they could to seek out care for John, including visits to an unorthodox apothecary who lived in the forest. Rose, the apothecary and beloved friend to all, is perhaps the most kind and caring inhabitant of Warren Hollow. She holds a lifetime of knowledge in healing and management of sickness, aiding anyone who seeks her assistance out in the forest. Aside from her God-gifted healing practices, us children view Rose as a friend and a wonderful individual. Rose is a free spirit who pays no mind to the growing judgment received from nearly everyone in our village. Unfortunately, Rose was labeled a servant of Satan for her ability to cure and banish illness without explanation, so she was taken to the prison but a few weeks ago. Accusations attack outliers and seemingly anyone who does not abide by normal behavior, so Rose was a prime target from the start. Mother and Father claim Rose to be the sole reason John survived his ailments at birth, and regular visits to her home in the forest continuously ensures John's stable health, year after year.

Mother lays eyes on me and her expression suddenly changes, in a way that signals a desire to end the current debate with Father.

"Emelie, dost thou arrive with an appetite for supper?" Mother asks in an uneasy manner. She attempts to conceal her emotions, yet I have always had the ability to see directly through her sentiment. Their marriage troubles have become much more prominent to me as I mature.

"Yes, Mother," I answer hastily, "I fear starvation is near if we do not go inside at once."

Father smiles at my remark and the atmosphere begins to lighten around us. While their relationship is complicated, and they brought me into this world at quite a young age, perhaps the only thing Mother and Father love more than each other are their children. As I continue to mature, my appearance is nearly identical to that of Mother's. She has been confused as my older sister on more than one occasion, which is always a good laugh and a compliment to her beauty, but the resemblance is truly astonishing. We share dark brown hair and style it identically. I have also inherited her bright blue eyes, facial features, expressions, and her near-perfect smile. On the other hand, John is but a mirror of Father, sharing the same humorous enthusiasm and curled hair. Father is a large man, full of muscle and strength from the hardships of farming.

Our home has been full of love and nourishment since the days of which I cannot remember. Tension can rise high at times, but feelings of care and happiness flow throughout the walls of our home. It appears we are the last family with rationality in a colony full of fear, torment, death, and treason for the slightest of actions. 'Tis true that we all live in fear, Father I believe more than he displays even to Mother, but once our doors close, we are still the same happy family as before the witch hunts and persecution.

As the sun begins to dim and lay for the night, Mother and I prepare a setting for supper while Father carries John to the table. John's eyes grow wide with excitement as he gets settled next to me.

"Sister! You must tell me of today's adventure in the forest," John asks excitedly. Mother also gains interest in the topic and begins to tell John of my misadventures.

"Thy sister would practically live among the trees if possible.

Since she was but your age we could never ease her desire for exploration," she says.

Mother speaks nothing but the truth. During the long winter months, I dream in constant of walking through the trees and becoming one with my surroundings. John shares a similar interest, as our secret forest gatherings have given him a breath of excitement into his debilitating life. John has remained loyal in his secrecy, as I fear Mother and Father may very well execute me if they discover our stealth in the night. The village could hold a mass execution if parents learned how all the children escape from their homes and gather in the forest to rejoice and engage in so-called wickedness. But it is a blessing for us all to forget the hardships we face at home and secretly celebrate together. We are scared, and gathering outside of the village makes life feel as though it is normal once more.

John's illness has hindered his development, restricting him to life at home as a cripple. I can sense John's desire to return to the forest with every question he asks upon my daily return. Perhaps I will share such a desire soon when Mother and Father prevent me from venturing beyond Warren Hollow's walls out of growing fear. In truth, it is my wrongdoing for involving John in my own sinful escapes. One night I was less furtive than necessary in my escape and John caught me dead to rights as I slipped past his bed. Rather than alerting Mother and Father, he simply wished to come along. And sure enough, the other children of the village reveled in his presence. John gets to live a superior life out in the forest, and in truth, I do as well.

As we continue to engage over supper, Father seems to commence a shift in tone before contributing to the discussion.

"Witchcraft continues to run rampant across all of New England," Father says boldly. I can feel the sadness and concern shining from Father as he continues. "Surrounding courts have begun to implement curfews for children and restrictions on exiting the plantations. Talks of doing the same here are soon to be enforced. I fear that the arrival of All Hallows Eve will bring nothing but disorder to Warren Hollow."

"But Father," I exclaim in revolt, "what am I to do if I cannot visit the forest? Are we to remain trapped in The Hollow, waiting until they enforce chains and enslavement next?"

"Enough!" Mother shouts in a tone forceful enough to command authority, but also to sympathize with my concerns. Us children refer to our mundane village as *The Hollow*, something that has always angered all the adults.

'You must speak proudly of our village; it is your birthplace and a vital farming plantation in the New England Colony.'

We all hear a similar scolding. Most of us have no interest in a life stricken to a farming plantation, a struggling and failing plantation to be specific, and will do anything necessary to venture outward.

Mother takes a moment and calms herself before giving an explanation. "It is for the best that Warren Hollow enforces such restrictions. Talk among our neighbors is growing, with accusations of children escaping into the woods under the full moon to perform rituals and engage in sinful adultery. Our association with the apothecary draws attention to us thus far, so it is wise for you to remain at home aside from chores."

But Mother, we are just seeking amusement! Is it such treason to dance with our friends by the fire and tell tales of hilarity while consuming berries and drinking ale? John enjoys these gatherings more than I! Shall we spend eternity in hell for living life the way in which we please? We wish not to care for crops or to spend the days exhausted in the sun completing chores that we despise.

Defensive thoughts race through my mind, yet I know better than to display any indication of our past attendance. John nervously meets my gaze in a way to signal both his fear and secrecy. We share full awareness of the punishment that would be brought down upon us if our truth was revealed. Although Mother and Father give us the freedom we desire, often more than any other children in the village, I believe this would bring a new level of repercussions we have yet to face. I attempt to envision a mild punishment from them, but they may very well put us on trial for witchcraft as other parents willingly allow for their children. My friends share whispers they hear from our parents at the church. The adults seem just as scared as any of us, and out of fear they will not hesitate to lock us up in the prison. Speculation and outlandish claims have resulted in Rose, a respected member of our community, fighting for innocence in the courthouse by day and facing cruelty in the dreadful prison by night. Perhaps they are fully aware of our past escapes to the forest, pretending to be asleep or ignoring claims of neighbors who may have seen us. Such actions would have been nothing more than a minor offense in the past. Or perhaps they do not hold such knowledge, regardless I shall take this as a warning. Mother and Father have not directly asked of my attendance so I will not provide any indications. All traces of dispute vanish from my mind, and we sit in complete silence for the rest of our meal.

II

A Growing Fear

A few weeks have passed since our debilitating discussion. Unfortunately, Father accurately predicted the state of Warren Hollow with All Hallows Eve rapidly approaching. We are but days away and our plantation is in total duress. Executions are in full effect with the neighboring trials, as lives are being taken for accusations of ritualistic practices, Devil worship, witchcraft, and irregular behavior that fails to meet community standards. Servants, children, and even respected individuals stand accused of practicing such wicked behavior. Nobody is safe from bewitchment, and if your name is spoken then you must be prepared to proclaim your innocence. Unbelievable claims continue to fly from the mouths of accusers, who perhaps act out of fear, aiming to place themselves on the safer side of the issue. For the first time I too feel fear and constant unease. The implemented curfew and regulations continue to tighten each day, with children no longer permitted to leave The Hollow for reasons outside of duty. Parents and officials face revolt from children who are brave enough to voice their thoughts and demand a celebration for All Hallows Eve.

Reverend Thomas instills fear into our parents through sermons that us children view as complete insanity. He was an arrogant and strict man prior, treating us as nothing more than sinners, enforcing his will through violence and fear. The word of God did not sound pure as it came from his mouth, so some of us have grown to dislike our time in the church. And with the recent occurrences, Thomas has seemingly lost all sense of his mind.

Witchcraft has yet to erupt within our walls beyond Rose, although I fear that it be closer by the day. 'Tis my hope that her innocence shall be regained and such commotion within our village will disperse. We are a close community, and I know for certain that none of the other children have engaged in these horrific behaviors. Regardless, Thomas continues to spread his word and enforce more regulations every day, with hopes that they will be broken. He has stepped forward and his power grows alongside his arrogance, without court officials or any political figures calming his efforts.

"Celebrations in any manner for this forsaken day are strictly prohibited in the eyes of God!"

"God will punish all who disobey and feed the desires of the Devil. We must first punish our children for their wicked behavior in order to repent."

"Do not let the Devil lead you astray, for he waits to tempt thy impurities and corrupt the minds of all."

Such wicked remarks are now expressed by all members of the village, especially from parents to their children after church service. Parents have begun to turn on their children, forcing us to engage in endless prayer. The Reverend has brainwashed them into believing us children as a conduit for the witchcraft that infests the colony. Most parents are now afraid of their own children, convinced that the Devil preys on our innocence and corrupts our souls because we have devoted our faith to a darker power.

Or so Reverend Thomas believes, while he knows not the first thing about any of the children of Warren Hollow. We enjoy prayer and all teachings of God, but we are afraid. Afraid of witchcraft and afraid of Thomas himself.

Mother and Father have become more reserved over the past

few weeks as well. Happiness has seemingly vanished from our home, and I now fully understand the effect this crisis has brought down upon us. I have engaged in battle with both Mother and Father over the lockdown we now face. A few hours at most are given to venture from our home, yet I am prohibited from traversing any further than the brook to wash clothes. In truth, the only happiness in life is now my daily chores. This is the only permissible interaction among us children and the only way to receive the solitude and peace from reality that I desperately long for.

Banishing these thoughts from my mind, I join the other children who also wash clothes in the stream. While we stand on the cusps of maturity and adulthood ourselves, we are still viewed to be nothing more than children, unprepared for any responsibility beyond simple chores. My dearest friend, Thomasin, smiles at my arrival as I approach the water.

"Hello, Emelie," she states with excitement, "hath thou faced punishment for conjuring up the Devil?"

"It is you who will bewitch all of Warren Hollow through your dancing and wicked behavior by the fire. They will hang you by the neck if you do not confess at once," I reply.

"So be it, we must gather the rest of our coven and curse this god forsaken village."

We both laugh and continue to make light of the situation in a playful manner. Thomasin is undoubtedly my closest friend, more like a sister, as we have known each other since our birth. She can be a bit of a troublemaker in The Hollow, taunting the boys with her beauty and always convincing me to engage in trouble as well. 'Tis true that we could be mistaken for sisters as well, aside from her bright blonde hair and impressive height, in comparison to my miniscule stature. Regardless of all the troubles she has caused me over the years, we are bound to each other and truly enjoy our friendship. All of us children feel safe together and share a connection that our parents do not understand. It is a bond held by all, and the darkest of times cannot halt our desire for freedom as we mature.

"Hath thy brother managed well with his ailments?" Thomasin begins to speak in a more serious tone. "These times cannot be easy for your family, and I hear whispers of a trial for the apothecary. Perhaps she will be labeled the witch of the woods as Reverend Thomas suggests."

"John is well," I tell Thomasin in an optimistic manner, "he has remained stable without his treatment that is since forbidden. Mother believes it is prayer that helps John each day. But I know our friend Rose be no witch, she is a gifted healer and one of the kindest souls of The Hollow."

"So, you do not feel the same as thy mother about prayer or these horrid accusations?" Thomasin asks sharply.

"Aye too engage in daily prayer for John, but doth mere prayer hold the power to heal a sickness stricken on John from birth? 'Tis Rose's wonderful treatments out in the woods that allowed John steady health. And in turn, my hours of prayer are met with silence."

Did I just openly question my faith or the power of prayer? How would Mother and Father react to the statements I have expressed? How will Thomasin react? Perhaps I too am corrupted by this witchcraft tearing apart our world.

Thomasin pauses for a few moments before providing a response. "Aye, my mother has spent night after night in endless prayer, yet our village continues to worsen. Even I have begun to question my faith at times. I am no witch, and I know for certain

Rose is no witch either."

I breathe a sigh of relief knowing I do not stand alone in my constant thoughts. Perhaps all children feel this way, our parents are so devoted to the church that Reverend Thomas fully controls their every thought. We do as we are told, and day after day our friends succumb to imprisonment and accusations.

"We are all pure in our faith," our friend Ezekiel proclaims as he approaches, "but innocent lives are being taken on account of foolish accusations. Would sneaking to the forest and having some fun match the viciousness of the Devil?"

Ezekiel is another close friend of mine. He is often covered in the dirt and filth of farming, and today is no different. Perhaps the only issue Ezekiel presents is his temper, as he is quick to defend any of us in the church or to adults, and never afraid to speak aloud the thoughts we all conceal. Shouting with the Reverend will often have him removed from service, which is always amusing. But Ezekiel assumes the rule as our so-called leader quite well, and he is a caring individual.

"Ezekiel, statements like that will have you struggling for breath in the center of the village," Thomasin jokingly tells Ezekiel as he sits with us near the stream.

"So be it, we are but prisoners in our homes and our lives have been taken away."

"I would give anything to walk the woods on this beautiful afternoon," I state in full agreement with Thomasin and Ezekiel as they go back and forth. "My brother longs for the return of our forest celebrations. But someone has spoken, and our parents know of such behavior."

"Perhaps you refer to our wicked bonfires of evil and

treason?" Ezekiel smiles before continuing the conversation. "We shall not wait for these days much longer, as the grandest bonfire soon approaches. I would like to invite you both to this year's All Hallows Eve celebration!"

Thomasin and I look at Ezekiel as if he has lost his sanity. There could not simply be a worse idea devised, given our situation.

"Perhaps you fall to corruption as well. It be best for us to alert your parents of such madness," Thomasin replies as she continues to wash clothes in the stream, dismissing Ezekiel and his foolish plan.

"Nonsense. 'Tis true, it so happens that the fullest moon of the year will shine on All Hallows Eve. And what better way to celebrate than with our biggest bonfire yet? I have come to tell you of the plans and refine your dreadful day of chores," Ezekiel says.

I begin to enlighten Ezekiel of my Fathers words. "Perhaps you have forgotten the curfew we all face, along with the fear of All Hallows Eve itself. It would be impractical to believe we could sneak to the forest and gather without our parents noticing."

"This be no different than what we have done in the past. All the other children are to sneak out for a few hours and have a celebration in the forest. They talk of creating masks and decorations appropriate to All Hallows Eve, so we shall honor the day like never before," Ezekiel claims.

Thomasin now scoffs at the idea. "Have you also forgotten about the accusations surrounding us? The murder and crimes of witchcraft? The slightest of odd behavior will have anyone in chains and facing execution. Let alone on the most feared night of the year."

"Our parents will not discover the plans, and if so they will punish us with nothing more than chores and prayer. Such nonsense may surround us, but it will not find itself in our peaceful little village. There be no evil witches or Devil's servants here. This night is exactly what we need during these dreadful times."

Against my better judgment, I cannot help myself from starting to agree with Ezekiel. Perhaps this is the worst idea I have heard, but I truly yearn for a trip to the forest more than they could ever fathom. Life has become a miserable mix of constant prayer and chores, and I know John would implode with excitement over the idea. Not only would this be an incredible celebration, it would also honor our favorite day of the year.

Ezekiel rises to his feet and prepares to walk away. "Consider joining us for the best night of your lives. We shall travel further from The Hollow and deeper into the forest than ever before. I hope to see you both there."

He leaves the stream, quickly turning and shouting one last remark before walking out of sight. "All Hallows Eve is a night to be celebrated!"

We both laugh at his idiocy, then suddenly Thomasin halts her progress on washing the clothes.

"Emelie, it pains me to say it but Ezekiel is right. I must get away from this monotonous existence, even if it be for a few hours in the night," Thomasin says.

"But what of the punishment we shall face if our parents discover our actions? This is a dangerous time and I fear even our parents could turn against us if we were caught in a situation so prohibited. Thomas has them fearful and ready to act!" I speak in a way to make Thomasin reconsider, but I sense she will not give in and perhaps I do not want her to.

"I will not sit here and face ridicule for wanting to be free. We have gone to the forest many times without the slightest indication of our parents' knowledge, so this time will be no different. We are nearly adults. Do what you will, but I must join them out there, and I wish for you to enjoy this night as well. And Emelie, Samuel and Henry will certainly attend as well. Perhaps I should go tell Henry that you hope to see him there," Thomasin explains in jest.

"You are to do no such thing!" I reply wittily as I grab her arm.

We both laugh at her closing remarks as she fights me off. Samuel is a close friend of ours, but very close with Thomasin in honesty. They have maintained an amorous relationship since we were younger than John. These actions are forbidden, but that does not stop any of us from engaging in such behaviors. And Henry is known merely as the son of a drunken farmer, banished from their far-away home for his father's conduct. Although most of our parents give him little respect because of his family name, Thomasin and I have grown quite fond of him and consider him a good friend of ours. I hold suspicions that he desires a closer relationship with me as well, although it has never been explicitly expressed. Thomasin often teases that Henry and I are destined to be together.

Thomasin hastily leaves the stream and I sit alone in contemplation. My instincts beg me for no consideration of the forest celebration. I understand that attendance would put my life, as well as John's, in danger. Though it is with difficulty to suppress this urge that claws its way from my heart.

What is but a life stricken to chores and nothing more? We do as we are told day after day and yet our lives crumble under our parents' fear. The Devil has never tempted us and there be not a single witch in the village. Can anyone comprehend that we simply desire freedom and excitement? What is a witch but nothing more than someone who finds the bravery to pursue the freedom that every single one of us covets?

I could lose my sanity over this newfound inner turmoil. Unfortunately for Mother and Father, I feel the desire to attend prevailing. It may be sinful, and the stakes may be significant, but nature is the ultimate force that guides my life to this very day. The forest brings me peace, not once judging me or enslaving me inside any walls. Within the deep woods I truly feel alive, and that passion has since been absent during the grandest time of year. What better way to recapture the feeling than with a celebration under the full moon on All Hallows Eve? This will truly be a magical night, never to be forgotten.

As I finish my chores and leave the stream, I hear whispers of plotting among the other children washing clothes as well. This idea quickly gains momentum and soon all the children of Warren Hollow will follow suit and gather in the forest. Strangely enough I begin to feel happiness and exhilaration for the first time in weeks.

Continuing down the path, I lay eyes on Thomasin. She stands in conversation with our friend Henry, staying true to her life's goal of making something of Henry and I. Slowly I move with a confident stroll as I approach Thomasin and stealthily inform her, "I shall see you there."

Thomasin and Henry match my smile, sharing the thrill and amusement that comes with acting in such a forbidden manner. I stop for nothing more than a few moments before continuing my venture back home. This excitement I feel is unmatched to the reaction John will have when I inform him of the plans. All Hallows Eve shall be a night to remember.

III

And So It Begins

"John, I have a secret that you mustn't tell Mother and Father. Can you promise me thy word?" I ask.

"I never tell anyone our secrets, sister, what is it?" John replies.

I smile, pulling myself closer to John in order to whisper in his ear. The time has come to inform him of this year's All Hallows Eve plans. Although it may be unwise to expose such a secret, 'tis my wish to bring joy back into my brother's life and fill him with excitement.

"It has been far too long since our last adventure," I begin, "but we shall not wait much longer. In secrecy, the others plan for a massive celebration on All Hallows Eve."

"All Hallows Eve!" John shouts happily. I cover his mouth with my hand, afraid that Mother and Father may discover the plans and punish me severely.

"Yes, John, but you cannot tell anyone. This is a big secret, and it is quite dangerous. With all that is happening in our village we must act with caution."

"I promise, sister, I will not speak a word. Oh I am so excited!"

Watching my brother regain his joy is truly a wonderful feeling. John faces hardships due to his illness each day, so it brings me satisfaction to know that I can provide him the ability to feel conventional. And he is always true to his word, never exposing our escapes or secret occurrences with Mother, Father, or anyone else. In the past, Mother was often hesitant in giving me permission to take John beyond the walls of the village, let alone out of eyesight from our home. Her worries are something I deeply understand, as his health has declined in the past and could worsen at any moment. Sometimes he struggles to breathe, but no medicines or healing practices bring him the relief that laying in my lap ever has. During his periodic bouts of worsened illness, I often spend the day laying by his side or cradling him in my embrace. We share an unbreakable bond that nobody else could ever understand.

Of course I began bending the rules, eventually bringing John to our first gathering a few years back. Rose was in attendance back then, so she watched out for him as well. While she initially disagreed with me bringing him along, she watched as the others welcomed him and eventually shared the same gratitude as I. In this mundane life it is necessary for everyone to enjoy themselves and escape from the daily struggles.

"We must leave in haste. Did you prepare your brother, Emelie?" Mother asks.

"Yes Mother, we are quite excited for whatever nonsense Reverend Thomas shall spout at us today," I reply.

John laughs at my words but Mother shows nothing but irritation. We are set to attend our usual service in the church, but recently the sermons have become highly arbitrary. Rather than expressing the word of God, Thomas now spends the hours shouting at us and scolding all for unjust behavior.

"Please do not dispute, Emelie. We must listen to the Reverend's words and fight this plague that spreads through the colony. Through faith he shall guide us," Mother says.

Father remains quiet, as usual, and makes his way outside

before us. I take a moment to fix John's hair and then we walk to the outside. Spending time in the church used to be joyful and informative. I often memorized the teachings so that I could strengthen my prayer and improve upon my sinful behavior. But now, Reverend Thomas treats us as though we are infinitely corrupt beyond reason and in need of punishment. With all the planning that surrounds All Hallows Eve, I am quite nervous to enter the church on this day.

Our way down the path is accompanied by nothing but silence. Mother and Father pay no mind to me and John, appearing as embarrassed or frightened to be near us in the public eye. Other parents act the same way, often making their children walk to the church alone entirely. 'Tis a troubling time, and it is hard to deny that tensions swell with every passing day. What was once a joyous retreat as a family has become dreadful. Yet I know it unwise to go against the words of the Reverend, for the punishment shall be severe. So I simply walk in silence like the rest, and conform to all of the increasing regulations.

Eventually we arrive at the church, a structure deteriorating from the harsh weather conditions we face. Warren Hollow is small and lacks the resources needed to completely restore the church, or any structures for that matter. I am grateful that our home remains fully intact and much more appealing than some of the others. Mother and Father have done quite well to repair any damages and maintain a functioning living space over the years. Apparently, that is not the case for most structures and homes of our village. The church is a fine example of true issues being ignored. This is a sacred place, but its current appearance reflects the ugliness unfolding on the inside.

We walk up the wooden stairs, which feel as though they

could break below me at any moment. Some friends pass as we enter through the doors, and everyone makes their way to the designated spots that many have held for years. Thankfully Mother and Father have found their place in the back of the church, which makes it much easier for me to hide and attract less attention than most. The normal greetings and cheer of service has completely disappeared, with families entering in silence, just like us.

I sit on the pew with John in my lap, Mother and Father following behind. 'Tis my wish that today's service goes quickly, and no issues arise. Cautiously I glance around the room, attempting to find any signs of joy and happiness. Though all I can see is fear, anger, and plenty of confusion. Everyone adjusts their view to the altar as Reverend Thomas aims to gain everyone's attention.

Something about Reverend Thomas has always bothered me, a feeling I have held since he came to our village but a few months ago to succeed the prior Reverend, Nicholas, upon his anticipated passing. Reverend Nicholas was a wonderful man, preaching in Warren Hollow many years before my birth. His old age made him susceptible to poor health, and sure enough, Thomas was appointed to our village merely weeks before Nicholas's death. Nicholas's teachings and operations were completely disregarded by Thomas the day he took charge. Perhaps it is the way Thomas holds himself that troubles me, full of arrogance and as though he be God himself. His long black hair often covers his eyes, and his height is intimidating. While I have never encountered Thomas outside of service, I do not enjoy watching him belittle my friends every time we enter these walls. Even before these recent events, Thomas was reserved and inhospitable since his arrival. Regardless, all our parents follow his every word, as he is now the sole Reverend of our small village. Nobody would dare to question the behaviors of Reverend

Thomas, fearful that they would be questioning their faith and God. So, he simply does whatever he desires, inflicting punishments on us and convincing our parents to do the same.

"Thank you all for joining me during these dreadful times," Thomas begins, "I'm afraid that I do not come with positive findings. All Hallows Eve draws near, and trouble shall follow. Before I speak the word of God, I wish to speak to the children. May all of you rise at once."

I look to Mother and Father, who meet my gaze sternly, nearly shouting at me to do exactly what Thomas says. Without hesitation, I begin rising to my feet, Thomasin and the others around the room following my lead. John holds onto me tightly as he tucks his head to my chest.

"Now, come forward to the altar," Thomas instructs. Although I sense something unpleasant awaits, I remain obedient and follow his instructions. One by one we make our way to the middle of the pews. The eyes of our parent's land upon me from all around the room and make me anxious, yet I focus on the floor and take apprehensive steps forward. My gaze remains low until I reach the pulpit. Thomasin, Henry, and Ezekiel stand by my side, with my other friends and the younger children directly behind us.

"What do you want with us?" Ezekiel asks. "Have we done something wrong?"

The parents gasp at Ezekiel's questioning remarks to Reverend Thomas. Rather than lashing out in reply, Thomas simply offers a maniacal grin and quietly scoffs.

"I am sure you are all aware of the troubles that surround Warren Hollow. Witchcraft troubles to be specific. Neighboring plantations are being devoured from the inside, all starting with the children. Now, I must observe you all, and ensure that this crisis has not found a way inside our walls," Thomas says.

And so it begins. These irrational accusations and occurrences have come to our peaceful village. 'Tis my hope that the others cooperate and prove this situation as erroneous. But Ezekiel has a temper, often becoming enraged when any of us are treated poorly.

"You suspect us of practicing witchcraft?" Ezekiel turns his attention to our parents. "And you all sit here and believe such outlandish accusations? For we do not even know what witchcraft entails," Ezekiel replies.

"Silence!" Thomas shouts, stepping forward angrily. "We are taking precautions to ensure your faith and purity!"

Our parents make no effort to calm the growing tension, although I fear that they would undoubtedly favor Thomas and whatever foolish methods he aims to present. He studies each of us, watching our movements and waiting for someone to display any guilty antics.

"I will ask questions, and you all shall answer," Thomas says while pacing the floor. "Now, do you all accept God and the bible?"

"Yes," I say without hesitation. My stomach turns at the realization that I am the only one of us who has provided an answer. Thomas stares at me for a moment before becoming enraged.

"All but one of you fails to recognize your faith?" Thomas asks.

"We are quite faithful Reverend, this is not necessary," Thomasin says tearfully.

Clearly Thomasin's words have upset the Reverend further, who slams his hand on the lectern. The younger children begin to cry from his actions as tension fills the room. Still I remain calm, abiding by his commands and wishing to be anywhere else in the world.

"It is absolutely necessary, for we must keep Warren Hollow safe! Now, do you accept God and the bible?" Thomas shouts.

"Yes," we all say in response.

"And do you accept all forms of prayer and your devotion to faith?"

"Yes."

"Hath any of you here today made a covenant with the Devil like the apothecary?"

"No."

"Did she teach you how to read and write so you could sign the Devil's book?"

"No."

The foul mentioning of our friend Rose has angered some of the others. 'Tis difficult for me to remain silent, yet I know now is not the time to revolt.

"Her name is Rose," Ezekiel starts once more, "and it would take a fool to think she is anything but innocent."

Please Ezekiel, all of you, if you would stay silent then we can save ourselves from this situation. I understand your anger, but we are in no position to act out of obedience. You are only feeding into his conviction.

Some of the parents begin to shout out and scold Ezekiel for his words. While I agree with his resistance, speaking in such dispute will further prove the suspicions of Reverend Thomas to be valid. If we comply and show that clearly none of us engage in witchcraft, then perhaps everyone else will begin to treat us like innocent children once more. Ezekiel has good intentions by defending our friend, but we shall join her in prison if he continues.

"You think conducting rituals and engaging with the Devil is innocent?" Thomas asks.

"Rose does not practice such outlandish behaviors, she is a wonderful person who many of you owe your good health," Ezekiel exclaims.

"Yes, she is wonderful indeed," John says happily with a smile. Quickly I place my hand over his mouth to silence his words. The others now begin to revolt like Ezekiel, which provides relief because I could not fathom the attention coming onto my dear brother. He simply does not comprehend the danger of our current situation. Lives are being taken elsewhere for so much as a suspicion of this behavior, which I fear may occur any moment in this church if the others do not calm themselves. Chaos erupts as parents try to reason with their children who angrily shout at Thomas and proclaim innocence.

"That is enough from all of you," Thomas yells, "let it be known that you all defend a sinful, corrupted heathen instead of respecting your Reverend. And unless you would like to join her in the dungeon of the prison, I suggest that all of you leave this place at once!"

Our parents begin to aggressively usher us down the aisle and to the front doors of the church. One by one we are forced outside, some falling down the steps and onto the ground. The doors slam behind us, with Reverend Thomas and all our parents inside.

The others begin speaking ill of the Reverend and his outlandish claims, shouting through the church windows and pounding on the doors. While I wish to join them in anger, I cannot help but feel an immense amount of fear as though this is only the beginning. We are now outside and will be completely unaware of what today's sermon shall entail after such an event.

"Emelie, what just happened?" Thomasin asks.

"I fear this is the beginning of something awful, Thomasin. Yet if they fully suspected us of witchcraft then we would be on our way to the prison," I reply.

"It holds no truth," Samuel says while joining our conversation, "we proved our belief in God and engagement in prayer. For those words could not come from the mouths of witches."

"I hope you are right, Samuel," I say. "I think it would be wise for us to leave this place!"

The others silence their agitation at my words, and suddenly I feel uncomfortable once more as all of their eye's land upon me. People who have never heard my voice are now staring at me for answers.

"We must stay calm and cause no disruption. Do as they say, and we will show them that there be no need to worry."

"That is smart, Emelie, yet I cannot watch as they speak ill of Rose," Ezekiel replies.

"I think it would be best for all of us to go home. And when our parents come, show them that you are engaged in the deepest of prayer," I instruct.

To my surprise the others begin to disperse and listen to my words. Most of them walk off angrily, but Thomasin stays right by my side.

"They listened to you. How do you remain so composed?" Thomasin asks.

I repeat the same question to myself, unsure of what exactly keeps me calm. Perhaps it is the knowledge Rose has passed onto me, how to manipulate my surroundings and remain one step ahead of the situation. Thomas asks for cooperation to his ridiculous actions, so in the moment there is nothing to do besides comply. We were granted the ability to walk out of the church, rather than thrown into the prison with Rose. Perhaps we have proven our innocence in those few moments, or perhaps they are devising a rational way to imprison us once witchcraft is fully understood. Regardless, I cannot show fear to John or anyone else.

"We must do as they say Thomasin, that is how we remain one step ahead, and also alive," I say as we begin walking down the path behind the others. "It is unclear how far they shall take these witchcraft accusations. Other communities across the New England colony are deeply affected, and it seems that none but the same has made its way here."

"I did not like what happened in there, Emelie. Our parents watched as he put us through such hell," Thomasin says.

"They are scared. None of us understand these troubles that surround us. My only wish is that Rose be free."

For the next few moments we walk without further discussion, watching as the others enter their homes as we reluctantly approach our own. Thomasin's home lies just before John and I's, so she gives us a final embrace with no further words before making her way inside. Now I walk the path alone with John in my arms. He appears unbothered and smiles at the falling leaves that blow in the wind.

"It is almost time for All Hallows Eve sister, and I cannot wait any longer," John exclaims. I am relieved that he remains joyful and puts no thought into the events that have just unfolded.

How could Reverend Thomas, or even our parents, expect these younger children to comprehend a crisis like witchcraft or to adjust their playful behaviors? It was frightening enough for the likes of Ezekiel and Henry, let alone these children only but a few years of age.

"Perhaps that is not a wise idea anymore, John. After today we must be cautious," I reply.

Thomas acknowledged the arrival of All Hallows Eve, so they will certainly watch for odd behaviors or breaking of rules. John immediately displays sadness at my words, the first thing to affect him on this day. 'Twas alarming to witness all of our parents supporting Reverend Thomas, making no effort to end his irrational assessment. While it is my hope that someone shall come to view today's events as absurd and put these growing concerns to rest, I still hold fear that the worst is upon us. The others will undoubtedly proceed with the All Hallows Eve plans, especially now to prove themselves and disobey Thomas.

"I will speak with the others and ensure that it be safe to leave the village that night," I tell John. "It would be a great risk, and after today I am not sure what punishment would await any of us."

"Then we must be extra quiet while we escape from our home!" John replies enthusiastically, wiping his tears and smiling once more.

Laughing at his suggestions and making a mess of his hair, I wish to diminish John's emotions no further. The dangers are now known, although we expected this to be our most difficult scheme in recent memory. Rose is no longer free to assist in the plotting or secrecy for such a gathering, so it is now our responsibility to attend the bonfire in the forest and assume all the risk. I hold no doubt that Rose would forbid any of us from sneaking to the forest on such a night. This is no longer a playful occasion with minimal punishment if we are caught. While precaution is always taken, I fear that no amount of preparation or vigilance shall hide our whereabouts on All Hallows Eve.

Ajay Bell

You understand that this night will be one of peril. It is not too late for you to change your mind, remaining at home without breaking the rules. But that is not what you want, and after today you still do not plan on following your own advice. So be it, but do not get caught. Nobody knows what punishment awaits for such an act.

IV

Into The Forest

The next few days come and go, nothing more than chores and prayer from sunrise until sundown. Reverend Thomas now holds private sermons for the adults, something none of us have ever witnessed in our lives. All children, from the youngest to the oldest, have been banned from the church until further notice.

Not something that draws any complaints from my mouth.

Mother and Father no longer engage in quarrels or even playful conversation, rather our home has fallen silent aside from the tearful prayers from Mother. All the parents and adults in The Hollow now treat us differently, as if we are demons walking through their homes, waiting to snatch their souls at any moment. Yet even with their suffocating supervision, our parents have no awareness of the plotting and preparations that have occurred out of their sight. We all share whispers during chores of how to escape. While much debate has occurred whether to diminish the plans entirely, this unfair lifestyle has pushed us further into revolt. Watching Mother and Father neglect John especially makes me ill and angry, and it is difficult to remain in compliance. Mother's hateful gaze never leaves me while I sit at supper or interact with John, and her presence is felt around the corner listening to every word of my daily prayers. I pretended to be asleep a few nights prior when she rummaged through my room, and I decided to avoid confrontation when I caught her doing but the same in John's area.

Undoubtedly, she was looking for any indication of a practicing witch in her home.

What are you hoping to find Mother? A poppet? Unnatural herbs used in ritualistic behavior? Perhaps some animal bones, fresh from a sacrifice? John cannot walk without assistance, but somehow you suspect he has found a way to bargain with the Devil?

The tension is certainly building, and though it may be for a single night, John and I must remove ourselves from such torture. When the moon shines fullest in the sky, I will act in my flawless manner of escape that has worked perfectly in the past. 'Tis critical to leave the window in the hallway opened slightly so that Mother and Father hear nothing but silence when the time to slip through arrives. John will pretend to sleep until I retrieve him from his area and straddle him on my back. We shall make our way out of the window, follow the trail behind our house, and sneak through the village's back gate.

And sure enough, the day has finally come. It is now All Hallows Eve and we are to have our grandest celebration to date. All the children in The Hollow are set to attend, with everyone making their own contributions for this magical night. A few children have ventured beyond the village walls and found a location deeper into the forest that is fit for our gathering. Many have created masks and decorations to honor such a night that we find so sacred. This day has burned in all our minds for months, and I have not seen such excitement for anything else in the past.

The oppression we now face has taken any joy or excitement from our lives. We believe that our parents have lost all sanity, and they have fallen so deeply into faith due to Reverend Thomas and his foolish teachings. Some parents have begun to accuse their own children of witchcraft and appear to fully support all punishments that may occur. Us children still do not hold the slightest idea as to what witchcraft entails, and I believe our parents do not either. Regardless, the most severe punishment for such practice is execution, and I cannot comprehend the idea of our parents willingly allowing these abominable consequences. Thomas acts in the way of an untamed beast, and we feel that he would certainly consider torture and execution as rational punishment.

Would my parents allow this for me or John? Would any of our parents really allow such a drastic solution?

The happy family that once shared love and compassion for each other has seemingly vanished from our home. Mother and Father have changed along with the current situation of The Hollow. Nothing has ever affected any of us to this degree prior to these witch trials. Life has always proven difficult, but Mother and Father shielded John and I from the troubles of the world. Regardless of outside occurrences, I have never felt the tension and panic within our home as I do now. Oftentimes we will eat in silence, and the welcoming atmosphere upon returning from chores is gone. Days pass without any communication. Any trace of our family rushing to the defense of Rose has departed. Perhaps Mother and Father now share the idiotic views of Rose as a wicked witch who aims to corrupt Warren Hollow and its surroundings. Each time Mother and Father return from the church it seems that they become more and more withdrawn from reality. I pray that they still look at John and I as their children, rather than vessels brought into this world to spread the Devil's corruption.

The unknown is my truest fear. Not knowing whether Mother and Father would send me or John into imprisonment if we acted in a way that did not uphold God's desires. But we are innocent young adults who enjoy mischief and amusement. Prior to these witch trials, a child would receive an addition to chores or a scolding from their parents. Now, punishments for identical sins may very well result in accusations of witchcraft and death. Mother's shifting thoughts on apothecary services directly reflects our current state in the colony. A few short weeks ago, Mother pleaded with Father to go and openly support Rose in the court, and now her alliance has vanished. Perhaps she conceals her support due to the fear that speaking out will lead to our persecution, but I believe that be the truth no more. Just like everyone else in The Hollow, Thomas uses the power of the church to guide Mother and Father's every move and think their every thought.

We all recognize the severity of celebrating on this night, especially due to the disgrace that has always surrounded All Hallows Eve.

"This is the night of the Devil! He shall roam free and corrupt the souls of all who give any observance."

In honesty, most children do not worry for the repercussions that we may face upon getting caught. We need an escape from this existence of pain and would do whatever is necessary to achieve it. Tonight will be no different than our many escapes prior, as any of us have yet to be caught and are all taking extra precautions. I debated with myself in regard to my attendance over the past few days, but the behavior of my parents and the direction life continues to follow has pushed me into my own path. I have nothing against the church or our faith, I even enjoy prayer and following the teachings of God, but the ordinance brought down upon our village and the innocent people on trial is not what God would have intended. Reverend Thomas manipulates sacred teachings to spread fear throughout The Hollow. All our parents, and the court officials as well, are so devout to faith that they will follow without question, and Reverend Thomas uses their credence for control and power.

A clear divide between parents and children has developed. They feel that us children are capable of conjuring demons and making covenant with the Devil, but we merely desire the civility that we once held. As the situation around us continues to worsen, it is now our responsibility to think freely and create our own future. We've all shared this lifelong desire for something more, and now is the time to act.

"God, please save our children. For they know not of the corruption that spreads through their souls," Mother states repeatedly in a tearful prayer as the hours of the evening grow upon us. I notice her sitting at the window, helplessly looking outward for answers as the daylight dies and night begins to ascend. Accurate to the words of Ezekiel, the fullest moon of which I can remember begins to illuminate the night. To remain anonymous, I bade it no mind and continue to clean from tonight's supper. Little mess has been made, as our meal portions gradually decrease day after day. Most nights I drift off to sleep with a growl in my stomach and an ache in my head. But most importantly, A few short hours separate John and I from the celebration we have anticipated so deeply.

"Sister, wouldst thou carry me off to bed?" John requests my service so that Mother and Father know of his position. I draw my attention to John, passing Mother as she tearfully recites scripture. Suddenly she grabs my arm on my way past, squeezing with enough force that I yell out of fear and pain. "You must engage in extra prayer tonight Emelie, for this is the night of the Devil!" She gives me firm instruction and aggressively releases my arm. Without saying a word, I continue walking to my brother.

I gently pull John up into my arms, and as I carry him out of sight from Mother and Father, we begin to discuss tonight's plans.

"Remember John, you are to not make a sound or cause any attention to yourself until I come and retrieve you," I say.

"And how are we to make our escape?" He replies quietly.

"Like always, John. We shall disappear through the largest window and scale the side of our home. 'Tis already open so it will not make a sound."

"But what about Mother and Father? Do you think they will watch for us tonight? What are we to do if they spot us leaving?" John begins to panic, and reasonably so.

If we are to be caught by Mother and Father, I hold no anticipation of their reaction. But it is too late to worry about the repercussions that we may face.

"Mother and Father will never notice our absence. We shall sneak from the window and return before they awaken. I have taken every precaution and hold faith in our success." I now lay John to bed as I raise my voice for Mother and Father to hear.

"Goodnight, John. Do not forget to state your nightly prayers. Sleep well, brother."

I give one final smile to John and leave the area to perform my own ritual of the night. I go through the motions of preparing our home for sundown, extinguishing the flames of the candles to diminish the last of the light. Mother and Father have gone off to bed and now I must wait.

The time grows near for our escape, and I sit in contemplation one final time before taking such a risk. Embarking on tonight's adventure may be dangerous and irresponsible, but I now hear the call of the forest through the open windows. It has been weeks since my last nature retreat, and the time to make my return draws near. While I feel excitement for the All Hallows Eve celebration, it is the return to the forest that excites me the most.

When more than enough time passes, I begin to creep from my bed and towards John's area. Complete stillness has fallen over our house, and I know it is time for our plan to enter motion. The large window is slightly opened like I ensured, so our descent outward should be nothing but silent. I stealthily make my way to John, watching every step in order to prevent Mother and Father from hearing movements directly above them. Full awareness of every creek in the floor is something I have long developed prior to our other escapes. Immediately I notice John's excitement gleaming all around him as I close in on his location. Signaling to me that he is still awake, I turn so John can wrap his arms around my back. This way I still have full use of my hands to make the climb. We have mastered the craft of escape by this point in time. Making our way to the window, I suspect Mother and Father are undoubtedly long asleep.

"Remember to hold on tight and watch thy head," I quietly remind John as I fully open the window.

The space seems tighter than in memory, but with John on my back I carefully climb to the outside. We begin to scale downward, and the wind blows my hair into my eyes. Winter is now in the air, and the coldness of our home burns my fingers upon contact with each descending step. Leaves pass by in the wind on our descent, and the smell of dying vegetation engulfs me.

What a wonderful time of year.

My feet hit the ground and I smile. This plan may in fact work like I have perfectly envisioned. As the chill of the wind stings my skin, I immediately feel rejuvenated and awakened. I believe that the late hours of the night bring the forest within The Hollow. The total darkness, chill in the air, wetness on the grass, and sharp silence tricks me into feeling like I stand deep in the forest. This night certainly appears to be the darkest of which I can recall, and it is time to hastily move onward.

Usually, we must avoid lit areas on our escape, but tonight that is not the case. The entire village looks abandoned, and I am overcome with a brief sadness while passing the neighboring houses. Some individuals have gone to the extent of boarding up doors and windows, and there are absolutely no signs of All Hallows Eve decorations. Typically, pumpkins and other organic vegetation lay on display outside most homes, but all that can be found is emptiness.

We venture onto the trail that leads directly out of Warren Hollow and into the forest. I begin to increase my speed as we move past the few houses near the village's back entrance. I recognize that the only light comes from farther away inside the church. This sacred place now fills me with nothing but disgust and anger.

Reverend Nicholas's service has proven exciting for me my entire life. He was a wonderful man, and I thoroughly enjoyed my time spent in the church. Faith brought us closer as a family and strengthened my relationship with God. But since his passing and the arrival of Thomas, the mere sight of this church now makes me fearful. I hope not to see the inside of those walls in the near future.

"You've done it sister!" Halting my thoughts and retracting me from my mind, John speaks in total excitement over the grand escape we have made countless times in the past.

"We are set to have a night of excitement that will not soon be forgotten. It has been far too long since our last gathering. Is't thou ready to celebrate this night of All Hallows Eve?" I ask John with excitement in my voice.

"Yes! I thank thee for bringing me along!"

36

"You are heavier than I recall John, perhaps your growth continues and you will surpass my height indeed."

"One day I hope to be as tall as Father, and it shall be Aye who carries my big sister to the forest."

John always remains optimistic and hopeful for his long-lasting health, regardless of being unable to walk and with growth that has stopped shortly after his birth. He continues to live happily and keeps an open mind at his youthful age. Nothing ever stops John from enjoying his simple life and feeling content in his own manner. All the children in The Hollow care for John and they will be thrilled once we arrive.

Since John's birth, I have taken the role of providing him with all the fun and excitement possible. Experiences such as sneaking out in the night to a bonfire would never occur for him otherwise. I find pride in my relationship with John and the fruitful life I get to bestow upon him in secrecy. Mother and Father take extra precaution with John, as his existence faces constant hesitation with anything outside of the house.

After a few minutes of walking in total darkness, I catch a glimpse of some other children who have also made their escape. I begin to follow them, as they will lead us to our destination. The children in front of us suddenly turn from our traditional route and follow a path that leads into the deep woods. This area of the forest is unfamiliar to me, as I do not recall a darkness so engulfing among the trees as we approach the new route. I find curiosity in this unknown path, and if us children have not ventured this way then I am certain the adults have not either. We are in unfamiliar territory, which proves as wise due to the likeliness of our usual space as compromised.

By this point we have undoubtedly ventured farther than

ever before in the forest. The Hollow is nowhere in sight and the moon is our only guidance as we move forward. Even I would be completely lost if this group of children were not leading the way. I do not believe we are on any path or trails, and how the others found this new location is puzzling.

Sure enough, light begins to shine in the distance as I push through the trees. Upon venturing closer, I start to hear voices and the familiar sounds of celebration. The smell of smoke from the bonfire encircles us and I realize that we have finally arrived at the All Hallows Eve celebration.

𝒱

All Hallows Eve

"Welcome Emelie and John! 'Tis a night of frolic and observance ahead of us, and we are all so jovial for your attendance!" Ezekiel formally greets John and I in an exaggerated manner as we make our way to the bonfire. "In order to honor this sacred night, you must choose a mask and wear it until All Hallows Eve's conclusion. But do remember, tonight the dead return to earth and the lost souls roam this forest!"

"Thank thee for such a glorious introduction, we will be sure to keep these dangers in mind. Perhaps the dead will take you with them at tonight's end," I reply sarcastically.

'Twas no lie about the scale of this celebration. The flames nearly touch the sky, and the landscape is fitted with decorations, food, drinks, and perhaps that largest gathering of children yet. John and I follow tradition and choose face coverings themed to All Hallows Eve. Mine appears to be a pumpkin with a foolish expression, and John's imitates a scarecrow-like figure.

"Emelie, 'tis the best thing I have ever seen. This is to be the greatest night of my life!" John exclaims.

"It is truly incredible John, look at the size of that fire. The flames burn my skin even at such a distance, and the decorations are beautiful," I say.

Children continue to arrive at our gathering, each providing offerings of pumpkins, candles, and various ornaments in honor of

39

All Hallows Eve. For the first time in weeks, I feel the happiness that has been fighting to break its way from the inside. I stare for a few moments in amazement at such a sight, and it officially dawns on me that I am back in the forest where I belong.

A group of children, led by our friends Henry and Samuel, approach joyfully at the sight of my brother. "John, we have not seen thee in the longest of time!" Henry proclaims.

"Hello Henry, it is great to see you all on this incredible night. I have carried John this long way, so I give to thee my All Hallows Eve offering," I playfully tell Henry as I give him my brother.

"We shall take him! What do you say John?" Henry takes John from my arms and begins to walk back to a large group of children who cheer at his arrival. I have always enjoyed Henry's presence, and although our interactions can be awkward, I do admire his care for my brother and his kindness. Perhaps he uses my brother to build a relationship with me, but John benefits so I accept it willingly. Thomasin often teases of how I speak or carry myself when I interact with Henry.

"Have fun, John!" I shout, but my brother is so engulfed in happiness that I doubt he hears my words.

My brother is to have a wonderful night with his admirers, and so it is my turn to find Thomasin and start my own fun. Sure enough I find her near the fire, which is typically her go-to position at our celebrations. Rather than a face covering, Thomasin wears a crown made of brush and berries.

"Thomasin, hath thou saved any ale for the rest of us?" I say in our typical best friend banter as I approach.

"You've made it," Thomasin embraces me in her arms and

continues, "and that mask looks divine on you. What really changed your mind, Emelie?"

"I could not sit at home in isolation while everyone else celebrated my favorite night of the year. And John needed this perhaps more than I. He is already having the night of a lifetime over there." I point to John who is smiling and enjoying the company of his friends.

"That is grand, Emelie. Although something has been troubling me since my arrival," Thomasin says with an immediate shift in tone. "This be the first celebration without Rose. She loves our gatherings and would bring the best berries and decorations. Now I feel a sadness that instead she sits in imprisonment, cold and alone."

"Aye, Rose would have loved the magic of everyone here tonight. She will regain her freedom and join us for our next celebration. We must visit on the day of her release," I say hopefully, but with inevitable doubt.

"Reverend Thomas hath gone mad. My mother struck me once we got home the other day for speaking out in the church," Thomasin begins to show sadness as she continues to converse.

I attempt to console her with my own experiences. "Life at home has drastically changed for us as well. Mother and Father have also fallen into the teachings of the Reverend, I have heard not a word from either of them aside from prayer. And it is hard to deny the feeling of division that grows between us," I say.

"These are troubling times, Emelie. Rose is just as innocent as every child here tonight. She will love to hear the tales of this night once she is free. If having frolic in the forest on a holiday makes a witch, then so be it! I shall be the most feared and powerful witch this village has ever seen. To hell with our parents and

Reverend Thomas and anyone not here on this night!"

We begin to diminish all sadness and attempt to enjoy the night that we longed for. I spend time soaking in the flames of the fire and listening to the wind blow through the trees. Sounds of laughter and amusement fill the forest and breathe life into the night.

This is the most beautiful area of the forest I have ever seen. I shall make this a permanent retreat for myself once Warren Hollow regains its sanity and allows exploration once more.

As the night gains momentum, children continue to arrive, each bringing additional offerings of decor, food, costumes, and contributions to this magical event. I converse with my friends and indulge in everything that All Hallows Eve has to offer. The moon beams down on our gathering and the fire continues to blaze for hours. Within these dark times that surround us, we have found a way to achieve happiness and take back the freedom that has been hastily stripped from our lives.

I look across this celebration and see nothing but smiles, cheer, and excitement. Contrary to the beliefs of the Reverend or our parents, there is not a child here conjuring demons, riding broomsticks and floating above the flames, conducting rituals, playing with poppets, or leading sacrifices to the Devil. Instead, we engage in dance and share tales of our lives with friends. As the children revolt and long for more independence, our parents face the fear of us committing sin or disobeying God. In turn, punishments confine us to our homes and strip our lives of joy. These witch trials gave the adults of the town total freedom to treat us as they please, and even the harshest of conditions are now acceptable. Perhaps they aim to ignore our maturity and treat us as nothing but children for eternity. If a dispute among neighbors erupts or a child acts disrespectfully, accusations of witchcraft are now a feasible solution to all problems. Parents deny their own wrongdoings in the upbringing of their children, so it is witchcraft that controls their every move and makes us sin or disobey God.

I believe that it is the officials of The Hollow and the church who belong on trial. They have fallen so deeply into faith and irrational fear that they have gone mad, and in secrecy us children continue to live a life of enjoyment and pleasure.

Thomasin is correct. If my newfound attitude and push for freedom label me as a witch then so be it, I too shall be as wicked as they come. The line between a hag in the woods worshiping Satan and innocent children who desire excitement has intertwined. Can every single child in attendance tonight be labeled as a witch? Even those who secretly continue listening to daily services through the church windows have decided to come, and their faith is perhaps the strongest of all.

As I continue to dance and interact with friends, an impending anger inside of me continues to build. I feel fury towards my parents, and the Reverend especially, for stripping our lives of these harmless experiences. The feeling that overtook my body upon our arrival is something I never want to lose again. Ezekiel spoke in accuracy, claiming this to be the greatest night of our lives. As time passes, I decide to make my way back to John and our group of friends. "Is thou behaving?" I ask in a teasing manner.

"Sister, this is the best night of my life. Thank you dearly for bringing me here!"

"Of course, John, this is just what we needed to make us feel better. But perhaps we should return home shortly."

"I wish we never had to leave, Emelie, we shall build a house in the forest among the trees and life off of this land."

"While I share a similar desire, we are to be thankful for one night away from the troubles at home. I promise the return of our normal forest adventures once these harsh trials are over. 'Tis time for us to depart," I tell John in a sympathetic manner.

I wish to stay among the trees and foliage as well, but I understand the repercussions of getting caught, so it is wise to soon depart. Still in no rush, I take John and embark on one final walk around the gathering and circle back towards Thomasin to say farewells. This celebration has rejuvenated all my emotions and provided me with a night of happiness and freedom. All Hallows Eve will not soon be forgotten by anyone in attendance. Without a doubt, tonight was the grandest celebration to date, and the number of children who came is extensive. We all poured our hearts into this, and it is safe to say we honored our sacred night to the highest degree. It pains me to leave, but as other children begin to depart, I feel this is our safest option before the sun starts to rise.

As I approach Thomasin, I notice her sharing a kiss with Samuel. I contemplate walking away but the desire to tease my dearest friend always triumphs rational thought.

"Gross! This adultery is not for our eyes, or any eyes for that matter," I joke with Thomasin and Samuel as I walk closer. "I see that Thomasin has bewitched thee."

"I'm afraid so," Samuel says with laughter, "your brother is a gift to us all Emelie, please bring him around in the village. He comes with the innocence and happiness that we all so desperately need," Samuel says enthusiastically.

"I shall, thank thee for watching over him and including him among the others. With certainty he will remember this night forever," I reply.

"Forever!" John shouts.

I now draw my attention to Thomasin. "And Thomasin, I thank thee for convincing me to attend. If anyone can make me sin it is you! I shall see you first thing in the daylight for chores."

Thomasin smiles and begins to show an appreciative tone. "What would an All Hallows Eve celebration be without the true witch of the woods herself? The desire of such a life has begun calling to me as it does you. I would love to join you and John when you continue those forest adventures."

"That would be divine, we shall recruit you when these restrictions are lifted."

Thomasin draws closer and suddenly pulls John from my arms. "Before you leave," she begins modestly, "I think you should give a proper goodbye to our dear friend Henry."

She uses her eyes to direct my gaze over to Henry, who currently sits alone by the fire. I try to pull John back into my arms, but she pulls away quicker, smiling and pointing in an aggressive yet playful manner. Suddenly I feel anxious, but also interested. We tease each other for a few moments before Thomasin begins pushing me towards Henry. I nervously laugh and ask Thomasin, "What am I to say?"

"Words, Emelie," she says as she forces my steps with another gentle push. I let out a deep breath and begin to fix my hair and adjust the mask on my face.

While walking away I nervously turn and tell John, "I shall be back in a few moments John, behave yourself!"

Thomasin continues to point and replies, "And you behave yourself Emel–"

Thomasin is interrupted by a commotion coming from the entrance of the gathering. Confusion falls upon me as I stop and stare aimlessly at the unfolding situation. Within the next few moments, our greatest fears erupt.

Children are running as they traverse past me at high speeds. Deafening screams explode through the forest and an echo of cries soon follows. I hear dogs barking and now piece everything together. The adults have found us. Shouting continues and children disperse in every direction, and I am aggressively knocked to the ground in the chaos. The forest begins to spin around me from such a collision, and a few moments pass before I regain control of myself. I struggle to rise to my feet, watching as they bombard the entrance and detain any children who fail to escape. Ezekiel rushes to the front, attempting to halt their entry but gets thrown to the ground. He is savagely beaten like the others who could not react. I stand frozen by the fire, trying to shake my dizziness while watching in fear as my friends are brutalized right before me. Henry's screams bring me down to reality as he rapidly approaches.

"Emelie, we must go at once! Collect yourself and move!"

"John! Where is my brother? Thomasin just had him, have you seen them?" I ask Henry in a panic.

"I am sorry, Emelie, everyone is running and making for an escape," Henry says.

"I need to find him at once!" I tell Henry.

Tears begin to fall as I search for my brother. I desperately look among the fleeing children and do not see anyone carrying John. The adults continue to detain the children, and those who do not cooperate are being brutalized until they submit. Gunshots ring through the air and children begin to climb over each other, even through the smoldering fire to escape.

What was a beautiful All Hallows Eve celebration has turned

into a battlefield in mere moments. Sure enough, I scan the area and spot John lying near a bush, not far from where Thomasin took him from me. He is crying and covered in blood as I quickly approach him.

"John, we must get away from this place! Are you hurt?"

"What is happening, sister?"

John is now in my arms, and I prepare to make an escape. I shield him as we traverse through the carnage that unfolds around us.

"They have found us, John. Somehow they discovered our gathering and found us. But we are going to get far away, and we will be safe!"

"Ezekiel is badly hurt. He put me in the bush and tried to help the other children. But they got Thomasin, and I fear they may have killed the both of them." John begins to cry hysterically from what he has witnessed.

"They will be alright, John. All that matters is that we escape and get -"

My words are interrupted as I am blindsided, receiving a devastating blow from behind once more. I drop to the ground and John lands next to me. Laying in a daze, my vision and the screams around me begin to fade. John struggles as he is picked back up, and I know it is not another friend providing aid. It is Reverend Thomas; he restrains John in his arms and looks down at me with disgust. Thomas mutters something of which I cannot comprehend to John and kicks me with enough force to send me into total darkness.

VI

Innocence Lost

uddenly I feel the sting of freezing water pouring over my face. Forcing a few deep breaths, I attempt to open my eyes in order to discover what is happening. Excruciating pain radiates throughout my head, and I succumb to an immediate dizziness. Lying motionless proves unwise, as I am once again drenched with water. This makes me sit up and identify my surroundings. Although my vision is blurred and I feel as though I am drifting down the nearby brook, within mere moments I recognize that I am in the church.

My hindered vision prevents me from fully identifying my attacker, although I recognize their outfit to be that of an official as they walk away. Only one of my eyes is of use, as the other is completely swollen and sensitive to the touch. Stirring memories remind me that I was attacked from behind, and then Reverend Thomas finished his assault with a crushing final blow. I sit recounting the events that have unfolded and immediately recall the Reverend taking John.

"John! Can you hear me?" I call to John in a painful and pathetic whisper.

Suddenly it occurs that I am not the sole prisoner of confinement. Looking around the church, I see that many other children who attended the All Hallows Eve celebration are also imprisoned. I attempt to stand, unaware that I am chained at the wrists and ankles. An unsuccessful struggle makes me accept that these chains prevent any further movement. The children in my near sight are heavily chained as well. Some are crying, pleading, begging for release, engaging in prayer, and others sit in complete silence.

"Emelie, are you alright?"

I follow the voice and notice that Thomasin sits close by. Without hesitation we attempt to embrace each other, but our confinement prevents us from coming in contact.

"Oh Thomasin, I think I may be seriously injured," I say as tears begin to fall.

"You do not look well, Emelie, yet you are alive and in better health than most. Some of the others did not survive the assault. Those in decent condition sit with us in this church," Thomasin replies.

"Have you seen John? I fear that he will not survive this on his own."

"He is not here with us, Emelie, the younger children have been separated and taken elsewhere while we remain. During the separation I did see John and he was unharmed. They restrained me back at the fire before I could make an escape with him, and for that I am truly sorry. It all happened so fast."

"There is no need to be sorry," I relax my posture as I continue, "I had him for a few moments before I too was taken. I must find him and further ensure his safety."

Thomasin pauses for a few moments before speaking nothing but the truth.

"I am afraid they will never allow such actions. We are now prisoners, our freedom gone and perhaps we wait for our death in these chains," Thomasin states in submission.

"But why are we in the church? Why is it that they took us

here rather than the prison?"

"We are not certain," Thomasin explains, "we have not seen Reverend Thomas since the attack and have faced interrogation from no one."

Why do they hold us within the walls of the church? Those accused of witchcraft are to be in the prison, so why does the Reverend hold us here with no explanation?

"There must be a reason for such imprisonment, I am sure the intentions will be clear to us soon. For now, we must wait and do as they say," I tell Thomasin as I surrender to a resting state once more.

All our fears have come true. We took great caution in the planning and escape to the forest, yet our parents and the village officials knew of our every move. I understood the risks of escaping The Hollow, yet I convinced myself it was for the good of John, rather than my own selfish intentions. Leaving the village was my only care, and I was willing to do whatever necessary to regain the feeling of freedom. Now John and I face punishment due to these unjustifiable actions. Perhaps our freedom would have soon returned once the neighboring witch hunts came to conclusion, yet we are now entangled in the chaos ourselves.

Hours of painful restlessness and suffering pass, until eventually I notice sunlight shining through the church windows. Although I feel better rested, the idea of sleep never crossed my mind. We are chained without comfort and grow more terrified for our lives with every passing moment. My head throbs from the pain and the significant damage enforced upon my eye now makes itself known. The church proves as frigid this time of year, and my torturous awakening has left me shaking.

Light begins to illuminate the church and I am horrified at

the sights that are now visible. Children sit in confinement across the entire church, leaving nearly no room to move or for personal space. The number of children imprisoned in the church is astounding, as nearly all the older children who attended the gathering are here. Some are in horrible health, with various children appearing to be badly injured, or potentially dead. Bruised and bloody faces stare back at me as I scan the church for my friends. Thankfully, Thomasin appears to remain unharmed, but I notice Henry and Samuel sitting together near Ezekiel and his condition is horrid. Ezekiel bleeds from open wounds and it appears that his final breath may be moments away. 'Tis my wish to give him my thanks for saving John, yet he may not recognize my words even if I were to break free and whisper in his ear.

A commotion arises near the church's entrance as I hear the door slowly unlocking. Children cry out as we all begin to sit up and observe. Light blinds us as the doors open. Reverend Thomas enters menacingly, with a look of pure disgust and also satisfaction on his face. He circles the room, holding a large wooden crate in his hands. Thomas slams the crate to the ground, shaking the floor with such force and breaking all silence. We all gasp and a few children break into tears, pleading for release.

"Let us go!"

"We have done nothing wrong!"

"You cannot hold us in these chains against our will!"

Reverend Thomas pauses for a few moments and begins to smile. He gazes around the room, and I notice his shining emotions of pride. Thomas is proud of the events that have unfolded, and holding prisoners in his church was perhaps a dream that he has turned to reality. No parents rush to contest whatever plans he has for us, and I know that we are truly in an unfortunate situation.

Walking around the room, Thomas lets out an evil laugh at the sight of our suffering and terror. He then makes his way to the pulpit and prepares to speak.

"Heed my words. 'Tis no longer of my control to justify your actions to God. You must beg for forgiveness and pray for salvation, yet the words of a witch will fall on deaf ears. Confess and perhaps you shall earn God's favor, otherwise you shall burn in hell."

We sit in complete silence for a few moments, which appears to anger Reverend Thomas. Perhaps he was hoping for revolt and panic, yet that was not the case. He simply smiles once more and walks towards the box that he brought with him. Hearing formal witchcraft accusations is terrifying, as the day that we all feared has come. This occurrence has spread like a plague, and finally to our peaceful little village.

"Now," Thomas announces, "you all enjoy making offerings to the Devil and celebrating his presence on All Hallows Eve. Thy plans of bewitching Warren Hollow will not succeed. Yet we shall continue the festivities and honor your master with one final offering."

Thomas reaches into the box and pulls out a face covering. The box is full of the masks and coverings we all wore throughout our celebration. A few village officials now enter the church at Thomas's command, assisting in handing us the coverings and releasing our chains so that we can rise.

"Listen carefully. Put on the mask of which you hold in your hands. God doth not want to see the face of a witch, so taking it off will result in severe punishment. Any attempt at escape will result in punishment, and any disobedience will result in punishment," Reverend Thomas says.

Children continue to cry and plead for mercy. My hands

shake uncontrollably as I peer down at my mask. Some children refuse to stand so they are being savagely beaten. To comply with directions, I put on the mask that is shaped to be a pumpkin.

Keep doing what they say. For any disobedience will end your life right here in this church. Follow along with whatever evil plan the Reverend has if you want to see John again.

The officials arrange everyone into a line and chain us together at the wrists and ankles. Any attempts to escape would be unwise and impossible. We are now slowly being led out of the church doors. Perhaps they are moving us to the prison or somewhere more suitable for prisoners of this magnitude.

"Emelie," Thomasin whispers in my ear, "I am so frightened."

"Aye as well, yet we must do as they say. Whatever Thomas has planned for us is clearly a test of obedience so we must obey," I whisper.

"How can they do this to us? We are innocent."

"Not anymore, Thomasin, we are now witches on trial for our lives."

The words stun me as I speak them aloud. This situation now fully engulfs me, the danger we now face fully sinking in. We are now labeled as servants of Satan, and we know that all witches shall hang. Stories from neighboring hamlets were merely tall tales and fables to us, but now we stand in perhaps the largest witch trial to ensue. Our lives hang in the balance, and proving innocence will be a near impossible feat. The only way to survive is through confession and begging for the forgiveness of God, Reverend Thomas, and our parents.

I pass through the large doors of the church and shield my

face from the burning sun. The brightness blurs any remnants of vision for a few moments and my head throbs once more. Slowly adjusting to the light, I notice how tremendously the temperature has dropped in these morning hours. The air stings my wounds as I continue to walk forward.

"Where are you taking us?" someone asks fearfully.

"Silence!" Reverend Thomas angrily answers.

Where are any of our parents?

After walking for a few minutes, I realize that we are moving towards the center of the village. 'Tis difficult to see given my impaired vision and the masks we are forced to wear, yet I continue without any complaint. Our surroundings indicate that the entrance of the prison is near, yet we pause prior to reaching the doors. Children in the front of our assembly begin to call out and move frantically. I am chained closer to the back of our line, so my view is hindered. Cries for our families hit my ears, and I notice a gathering of parents standing motionless near the center of the village. I desperately scan the area looking for Mother and Father, yet I do not locate them in the crowd. No parents make any attempt to console their children or free us from these chains, so my fears are further proven as accurate. Our parents are too far gone into the Reverend's teachings. We were never to be saved because our parents also believe us to be witches, taken by corruption. The mere thought of my parents supporting this brings tears to my eyes, so an effort is made to ignore the crowd for the fear of successfully locating Mother and Father. No longer do I wish to see them. Reverend Thomas makes his way to the front of our line and onto the small platform in place under the largest tree in The Hollow.

This beautiful area always brings me the same peace as the deep forest. I remember sitting under this particular tree for hours, watching the wind blow the dying leaves to the ground and smelling the scents of autumn's arrival. This area was my only escape to nature while our village walls remain closed.

The sight of Thomas on the platform brings us all to complete silence. Our parents remain still, and a feeling of uneasiness washes over me as if we are about to witness an unpleasantry. Thomas raises his hand as he prepares to explain his reasoning for marching us to The Hollow's center.

"Observe," Thomas says sternly.

We wait for more context, yet Reverend Thomas speaks not another word.

"Observe," Thomasin whispers, "what are we to observe?"

"I do not like this Thomasin, for I believe we are to bear witness to something horrid," I reply.

Thomas aims his sight to the group of officials, who use his signal as direction to begin their motions. Sure enough, the men walk around the corner of the prison to retrieve whatever Thomas desires. My hindered view causes me difficulty, yet I distinguish the officials marching back with someone else to the stage. Staring in horror, I recognize the attire of the prisoner. It is Rose, the apothecary. Her face holds no recognition, as she shows signs of torture and brutality. Her appearance indicates that she has been kept in a dungeon or torture chamber, and in horrid conditions. Rose walks slowly as though every step causes pain, and the officials must provide her with support as she makes her way to the platform. The joyful and beautiful Rose does not deserve such torture, and her imprisonment appears to have deteriorated her life.

I now understand what we are witnessing. Rose has reached the end of her trial, and Reverend Thomas wants us to observe what the future holds for all of us. Thomas smirks at the sight of Rose as she struggles to climb the platform. She makes no attempt to escape or revolt against her captivity, as she simply has no struggle left in her.

"Today," Reverend Thomas begins, "we gather to conclude the trial of one Rose Adie. Rose, you face conviction on proof of witchcraft and treason. For Satan granted you the ability to heal and cleanse and you accepted his power without dispute. You live a life of mystery in the woods, communicating with the vegetation and controlling the wildlife to do your bidding. The corruption of all children in Warren Hollow begins with you, as these ritualistic practices hath corrupted our children. What say you in this final attempt of forgiveness?"

Rose never raises her eyes to the Reverend, rather, she stares blankly at the ground beneath her. Appearing as if she may fall at any moment, Rose starts taking steps past the Reverend and raises her view to us children. She becomes emotional at our sight and attempts to speak out as the Reverend grabs her and pulls her back, so they are face to face.

"I ask thee one final time," Thomas shouts, "confess!"

"I -" Rose pauses and finally raises her gaze to meet Reverend Thomas's. "I am no witch. You know this, Reverend. Better than anyone here today. There be no witches here. 'Tis true that I am a healer of sorts, relying on nature and simple techniques, with no involvement of magic or evil. I have saved lives and brought peace to many of you here today. Still, you condemn me as a witch. Yet I am no witch, and I shall not make false confession. I do not confess," she says.

We all gasp and panic at these unfolding events. Thomas angrily pushes Rose to the ground and signals for the officials to start the execution. We begin to plead, begging for no harm to fall upon Rose. Some try to scale the platform and reach out to Rose, yet she makes no attempt to escape or halt the punishment before her. I begin to cry and shout for her safety, but I do understand the choice that Rose has made. Some people would immediately exclaim false confession to save their lives, but Rose will not, and understandably so. She has acted as a vital member of our village, healing many and providing care to banish illness and fight disease. Rose solely saved my brother's life and assisted in his development for years until this unjust imprisonment. Her work is of prideful regard, so a false confession would dishonor her gifted abilities and everything of which she prides herself upon.

How can they be so blind and oblivious to assume Rose as a witch? She is an apothecary who excels at her work. Life in the forest has granted her the skills of utilizing nature to develop remedies. She is innocent, perhaps more innocent than anyone in The Hollow. Mother pleaded for her safety, yet now Mother will cheer for her execution.

The officials fix the hanging rope around the tallest branch of the tree, and they subdue Rose to place the noose around her neck.

"Rose Adie," Thomas formally begins, "I sentence you to death. Doth thou hold any final words? Perhaps a final plea before condemnation to hell?"

Remaining composed, Rose takes one final look at the parents and then us children.

"It's not aye who shall venture to hell, nor any of these children facing false imprisonment. God shall pass my final judgment, so kill me if you must. My innocence shall carry until the end of time. I have saved lives, and if that makes thee a witch then so it be. Yet killing me will not tame the desires that burn within these children. The days of old are no longer upon us, as they will settle for manipulation and condemnation no longer. And to all of my children here today, I urge you to live by your own desires. If I am to be a witch, Thomas, then you shall be the Devil here before me."

Reverend Thomas strikes Rose with a devastating blow, clearly angered by her words. He does not care to hear any further sermon, and signals to proceed with the execution.

"All of our truths shall be revealed in due time," Rose says, offering one final phrase of her wisdom with a subtle smile as the tightening of the noose ceases her breath.

Rose closes her eyes, preparing for her life to end in full submission. Two officials stand behind her, establishing a grip on the rope to lift her vertically. Silence falls over us children as we watch in horror.

Thomas gives the final signal and Rose is lifted high into the air. Rose begins to struggle frantically for a few moments, reaching for the rope around her neck. I decide to look away, as the sight of my friend's death is unbearable. The others make their final pleas and attempt to stop the execution, but 'tis of no use. All signs of life begin to fade from within her, and Rose is now dead. A fate that I fear awaits every one of us.

VII

Covenant

We stare in horror at the lifeless body that was once our dear friend. Reverend Thomas also watches, but with shifting emotions. Rather than laughing and staring with pride, his expression reflects fear and potentially regret. Thomas attempts to conceal these emotions and draws his attention to the crowd. The entire interaction between Thomas and Rose felt as though it was more than a simple execution. This struggle to regain composure and Rose's articulate words are leaving me bewildered. Nonetheless, the others continue pleading for mercy. I know that will be to no avail moving forward, so I do not give Thomas the satisfaction of watching me panic. Rose has been murdered, after weeks of court proceedings did not uncover her innocence. She met her demise over mere suspicions and accusations, so I believe a similar fate awaits us all soon.

"Children," Thomas slowly begins, "let this be a lesson to all. This woman danced with the Devil and refused redemption. We pleaded with her to confess, yet she would not. So her destiny was death. Let us hear thy confession, and through the teachings of God we shall save your soul. Otherwise, the Devil awaits you in hell."

Some parents finally voice their support for Reverend Thomas and beg us to confess. They promise salvation for our lost souls and shout for us to accept God back into our hearts. Every parent here today fully believes that Rose was a witch, and we are now bewitched as well.

How can they witness an innocent person's death and scold us as sinners and witches? They watched pridefully as Rose was killed before our eyes, yet we are deemed the ones who lack sense and need forgiveness.

Ezekiel pushes his way forward and begins to shout at our parents. "You all need beg for forgiveness. You shall slaughter us on false accusations and follow a monster who seeks benefit for himself. There be no witches amongst us," Ezekiel proclaims boldly.

"Silence creature! You shall hang at this instant otherwise," Thomas shouts in response. "You all must stand trial on accounts of witchcraft and Satanism for thy ritualistic behavior in the forest. Attempts of escape or deception are quite unwise. Through confession and cooperation, you shall receive forgiveness."

Officials signal our movement forward to the prison. To reach the destination, we must pass our parents along the way. I fear the sight of Mother and Father, so I aim my gaze to the ground, focusing on my steps and the broken gravel.

Why do this to thy children? Doth thou truly believe we are witches who conjure spells and fly through the night? Perhaps some of you still have sense among you, yet doubtful I be.

Sadness manifests into anger as we lose sight of our parents. We approach the menacing doors to the prison, and Rose's condition instills me with fear. Her body displayed signs of torture and mistreatment, with death appearing as a relieving escape for her on the platform. She would rather die than return to this prison and falsely label herself as a witch. And I do accept her choice as reasonable. The truth behind freedom and redemption after confession is unknown. Would a confession simply release us back to our lives of normality while those who do not confess are murdered? Rose put little faith in the promises of Reverend Thomas and accepted that death was imminent either way. While Rose willingly gave her life before us, her pride and bravery shall live on through each child imprisoned today.

We enter through the doors of the prison and an unbearable stench greets our arrival. The poor conditions of this structure are noticeable after mere seconds of standing inside, but this is to be my home for the time being. Our masks are finally removed and officials usher us down to the basement level. Light departs with every step as we continue our descent. Torches and lanterns provide the only light to this area, although I notice that cells have a small window to the outside as we pass through the narrow hallway. Mice and rats disperse at our arrival, and the floor holds puddles of filthy water. Children are now disbanded and placed into cells as we pass, typically two children at a time. Ezekiel and Samuel receive the first cell by the stairs, and this process continues as we make our way down the dark and intimidating hallway. The barred doors slam behind children as they are unchained and forced inside. Some attempt to escape and are met with brute force until they succumb to their fate. Now is not the time to plot an escape, under no circumstance would breaking free find success. I understand the defenseless position in which we find ourselves, so I obey the Reverend and cooperate to remain unnoticed.

Eventually it is my turn to enter a cell, and I find relief to see that Thomasin and I shall face confinement together. Our cage closes and we immediately embrace each other.

"I am so scared, Emelie. We are to die in these walls. This place sucked the very life from Rose and now we wait to meet our death as well," Thomasin cries.

"We will not die, Thomasin. We must find a way to escape, and we shall give them cooperation until we do so. 'Tis unlikely we will face execution first, so we shall see if the promises of freedom from confessions are true, although I doubt that as accurate. And I am in no condition to make an escape, so we must wait and begin our plotting," I reply.

"Rose was a single prisoner held here for weeks, Emelie, and now all of us fill this place. We will live here for years as they try us all, yet I fear that none of us shall survive that long based on Rose's condition."

"Perhaps a few months, but they cannot feed us and house us all for years. These trying times may pass rather quickly if word of Reverend Thomas's actions spreads. Perhaps someone will come to save us. And they will not execute us without trial, or else we would have met our death alongside Rose."

We begin to fix our cell, although our efforts bear little results. Our cell holds two makeshift beds of quilts and hay, along with a bucket for relief and a small window. There be no protection from the outside weather, only a few bars to prevent our escape. Something that causes concern as the nights will inevitably continue to grow colder.

"The window, Thomasin. For what does our view allow?" I ask desperately. Thomasin makes her way to the wall, using our chamber bucket as leverage to look outward.

"The hanging tree is just within view, and Rose's body is still there. 'Tis my hope the younger children did not witness such horrors from their confinement," she replies.

John. How could I have forgotten about my brother?

The younger children were not present in the church, so they must be on the other side of The Hollow in the smaller prison quarters.

"If any children are moved, then we are sure to witness it all," Thomasin says.

I draw my attention back to the inside of the cell, now noticing that we face our two friends, William and Robert. William is one of the oldest children in the village, practically an adult himself, but still a good friend to us all. He has always been pleasant in our few interactions during chores or after church service. Robert on the other hand is a friendly individual, but a known troublemaker. He is often heard in dispute with his mother and father over breaking rules or causing issues. Robert has been forcefully removed from the church on more than one occasion for disruption and mockery. But we all find him amusing, which is perhaps why he proudly fills his self-proclaimed role of village idiot so well. Although I am not as closely acquainted with them like Henry and Samuel, I know that we must get along and cooperate with everyone if we are to make an escape.

"William, can you hear me?" I ask timidly. "It be Emelie and Thomasin."

"Emelie, it is good to see you, although the circumstances are not great," William answers.

"Are either of you hurt?" Thomasin asks.

"Thankfully not, yet we both took a beating in the forest. We almost made an escape, but it was simply too late," Robert replies.

"We must remain calm and wait for the moment to arise in which we can make an escape. It may be days or months beyond, yet the time will present itself and we shall have our chance," I tell everyone.

"But Emelie," William speaks up, "they shall kill you if such action is attempted. Reverend Thomas said the only path to freedom is through confession."

"And confession to what?" I angrily ask William. "There be no witches among us in this prison. How can we confess to something of which we do not partake? Our parents view us and the younger infant children to be full of evil. We could make a false confession of witchcraft, but I fear that the Reverend will slay us regardless. Rose knew the only way out of confinement was death, so she faced her judgment with pride."

Thomasin now rushes to me and pulls me closer to her. "So thy shall not make confession? Emelie, if you do not then they will murder you for certain."

"I fear that we are to die either way, and we must choose to die pridefully or as liars, if the conditions of this confinement doth not take us first."

Perhaps I am being stubborn or acting irrationally out of anger at my friend's murder. 'Tis hard to assume we will be safe after making a confession. Thomas is ruthless, only wishing to grow in power and kill us all. Witchcraft is merely an excuse for his horrid behavior, and worst of all, our parents do not see such truth.

"Perhaps you are right," William states in agreement, "who's to say Thomas will not hang us by the neck after a confession? But we must take your suggestion and obey his every word. These are your own words, Emelie. And look, we sit at the end of this corridor, so 'tis likely those near the stairs shall face interrogation first. It be wise to wait with patience and observe those who shall immediately confess. Perhaps they will obtain freedom, and if so, we must follow and do but the same. If confession does not save us, then escape by any means is our only choice."

William understands my concerns but offers rational thoughts on the situation. Remain silent and abide by rules to stay unnoticed, then escape at the first given chance. Within minutes of facing confinement, we have an escape plan developing. We must save ourselves in order to save everyone else. Although I do not hold pride for false confessions, this could give me the freedom to retrieve John and make an escape. John holds more importance than my own foolish pride.

We all stand in agreement throughout the filth and shadows of this dungeon. This cell shall be our cage, but it shall not be our tomb. Obedience is necessary until the moment to strike arises. I will wait patiently in constant thought, devising an escape strategy for us all. If false confession releases us, then I shall do so and retrieve my brother. If maneuvering out of the window or escaping through my cell door is the only hope, then I shall devise a plan like I have done in my own home.

Perhaps our way of life shall never be the same. If we discover a way to survive, The Hollow could not possibly return to normality. Yet, the only thoughts in my mind are escaping and finding John. I do not wish to reconcile with Mother and Father or convince anyone of my innocence. A plan must be formulated to perfection so that we can all escape with our lives.

VIII

Self-Condemnation

Weeks pass although it feels like years. The prevalence of darkness and a growing chill in the air indicate that winter has arrived. We shiver through the nights and soak in the few hours of sunlight that beam through our cell window each morning. Recent days come with snowfall just outside of our window, along with the certainty that a harsh winter will put an end to our survival. Each day grows colder than the last, as a mere quilt is the only protection we hold against nature. However, 'tis not my survival of which I fear. The sole thought that burns in my mind with every passing second is John. I pray for his safety and comfort wherever they hold those younger children. John simply would not survive the winter in the conditions we face, and his ailments will not allow him to remain in good health within confinement much longer.

Feelings of guilt and remorse slowly kill me in this cell as I sit day after day, staring at the empty walls and blaming myself for what John must now endure. If I acted responsibly and left him at home, then he would not face such cruelty. The torture I put myself through is far worse than anything Reverend Thomas could enact. Eating is a feat of impossibility when minimal meals are provided, as I feel undeserving of any self-satisfaction and willingly go days without consumption. I attempt to conceal my emotions and remain strong, as the only chance of freedom is to follow our initial plan. John shall remain in chains unless I am given the chance to confess or escape. Waiting patiently for either situation continues to fuel my rage and resentment. Perhaps if any of us were real witches then we could use our minds to break the chains and free ourselves. Though that holds no truth, and a village of innocent children shall die upon winter's arrival.

"Emelie," Thomasin begins, "doth thou remember our days of frolic last winter?"

"Ay, the snowfall provided us with weeks of merriment. Our chores halted so we would spend days walking on the frozen brook and building our own houses of snow in the forest," I tell Thomasin.

"Yes, we buried John in the snow, and he loved every moment. Remember our great snowball battle with Ezekiel and the rest of the boys?"

"Those were great times, Thomasin, I truly long to regain the freedom we once had," I say in a more serious tone.

"And I as well, what do you think will come of us, Emelie? Will we ever find freedom or survive through this torture? And if so, will life in The Hollow ever be the same?"

"I sit in constant with similar thoughts, and I fear life will never be the same. We may survive, although our parents do not deserve forgiveness for the torture they willingly let us endure. Mother and Father once cared deeply for John and I, now they let us suffer for outlandish accusations. I must retrieve John when the opportunity arises and escape into the forest. We shall find a faraway village and start a new life."

"That sounds swell, perhaps I shall do the same. The others may agree and wish to leave The Hollow as well. We could travel far beyond this place and grow a community. One where everyone has freedom to be themselves and happiness is our only care."

Although this sounds unattainable, I show support to Thomasin's positivity and agree. A place where we hold total freedom over our lives would be incredible.

"First we must escape this cell, Thomasin," I remind her, "then we will travel as far as we desire."

We sit for hours, fighting to stay warm and discussing the life of our dreams. One where children are not a slave to parents and faith, and we no longer suffer through endless chores to satisfy good will. Our future will come with freedom and celebrations of massive scale every night. If witches want to join us then they shall fly freely through the night, and every day can be All Hallows Eve.

You are going to die in this cell and you know it. How can you possibly achieve a new life if you slowly kill yourself day after day?

My thoughts begin to torture me once more throughout the night. My body shakes and my teeth chatter in my mouth. Thomasin and I have begun to share a mattress to keep each other warm under our quilts, although there would not be enough coverings in all of Warren Hollow to protect us from the harsh weather creeping in. Icicles form on our window, so perhaps it is later into the season than we initially speculated. 'Tis difficult to hold any accuracy of time in these walls.

How long have we been here?

These nights are the most horrid and unbearable circumstances I have faced in my life. None of us children deserve to go through such starvation and exposure to these conditions within the prison. Our wounds were never treated, and the prison smells of rot and filth. We all wear the same clothes that we wore to the forest on All Hallows Eve, with nearly all of us covered in dirt and blood from weeks past. The officials have yet to begin interrogations, so we wait in fear that they shall wake us in the night for execution instead. Although, my instincts tell me differently. I believe that Reverend Thomas was not prepared for his plans to fall into place. He was proud and arrogant that he convinced our parents to follow his word, yet at Rose's execution I witnessed his entire demeanor shift. Often, I recall Thomas's mischievous expression, one of near sadness, and ask myself why. He expressed an utter hatred for Rose, so why did her execution trouble him so deeply? The ultimate power of taking a life must have affected Reverend Thomas more than he anticipated. Perhaps he is devising a plan to undo his actions, or he may be rebuilding his confidence to execute us all at once. Never-ending thoughts of death and my fear for John prevent me from ever achieving rest. I often face delusion and exhaustion from my lack of sleep, which continues to worsen my overall health. My thoughts take shape and fill the darkness every night until sunlight peeks through the bars of our window, signaling the beginning of another day, identical to the last.

On schedule, the sun begins to illuminate our cell, indicating that we have survived another night behind these prison walls. As I rise from the mattress, I hear a commotion of noise coming from down the hall. I peek from our cell and notice the children panicking near the stairs.

"Thomasin, Emelie," Robert calls out anxiously, "they emptied some of the cells near the stairs!"

"What doth thou mean?" I ask Robert.

We begin to hear shouting and learn that a few of the children were taken prior to my awakening. Ezekiel and Samuel have been removed, along with other children in surrounding cells.

"Go to the window, Emelie. Perhaps we shall see where they take them," Thomasin instructs.

Rushing to the window, I empty our overflowing bucket to

broaden my view and locate our friends. I use my hand to brush away the icicles that have formed overnight, and sure enough I see the group being led by Reverend Thomas towards the courthouse. I must shield my eyes from the brightness of sunlight and the sting of the air. Light snowfall covers the ground, so it is early in the winter because the snow eventually submerges all houses and walkways in the village. The harshest snowfall often leaves us stranded in our house for days at a time, with Father only leaving the house if necessary to retrieve supplies or wood for the fire. Sometimes the fire inside my home would not provide warmth, so I fear what shall result from constant exposure to such conditions.

The group of officials and our friends disappear through the doors of the courthouse. I slowly step down from the bucket and use the quilt to wipe the snow and frost from my face. A few seconds of exposure to the outside has left my face bright red and sensitive to the touch.

"They entered the courthouse," I say loud enough for the children in surrounding cells to hear. "We shall take turns keeping watch for any signs of movement."

Thomasin and I take shifts peering from our cell window, searching for any indication of what is unraveling in the courthouse. We watch for what seems like hours with no movement. The weather begins to significantly affect my face, and Thomasin's as well. Both of us have developed a cough over the past few days, and I know our health will inevitably worsen as we get deeper into the harshness of winter.

"Someone will confess. 'Twas a large group and I know that given the chance I would confess until I could no longer draw breath if it meant leaving this cell," Thomasin explains.

While I think false confession is useless, the conditions that we face could break anyone. If offered a seat by the fire and some proper food, I fear that some of the others would start to turn and accuse the rest of us.

"And I as well. My fingers have gone numb days ago and this winter chill shall leave us frozen if we do not escape. I hold doubt for Ezekiel's confession, although the others will certainly confess or place blame upon the rest of us for bewitchment. This will show if there be any truth behind Reverend Thomas's words. Perhaps a confession shall lead to freedom, and these children may walk free from the doors of the courthouse. If not, then we follow our plan of escape," I tell Thomasin.

"All the time in this cell has provided me with endless escape plans as well. Although, an issue has presented itself that perhaps we did not consider in the beginning," Thomasin replies.

"What is it, Thomasin?"

"Winter is upon us, and I do not believe we would survive after making an escape. Our clothes do not provide protection from the conditions of this cell, so surely we would die facing the weather outside."

Thomasin is right. Enough time has passed and now the weather adds difficulty to our escape plans. If the chance to escape presents itself, we may very well die upon exiting The Hollow within hours.

"We would need to find somewhere away from the cold. Somewhere our parents or the Reverend will not discover us. Leaving The Hollow is our only hope, but we shall die without shelter," I tell Thomasin.

"Emelie, I know exactly where we could start our journey. We will not face the cold because we shall travel to a house, the only house outside of the village walls."

I match Thomasin's gaze and we both smile at the

developing idea.

"Rose," we say at the same time.

"Her home provided difficulty for most in The Hollow to reach before any witch trials began," Thomasin explains, "regardless, our parents wouldn't dare step on the land of a witch."

"We shall gather at Rose's home if we are fortunate enough to make an escape. She had endless supplies that could provide us good health," I add.

"Rose knew the forest better than any hunter in The Hollow, she would also have a collection of maps and materials that would further assist in our travels."

"We must pass word along to the others. Anyone brave enough to attempt an escape or follow our lead is to gather at Rose's home."

"It sounds like we now have a plan in pl-"

Thomasin gets interrupted by shouting from the others to look from our window. Without hesitation, I prop myself up and watch as the courthouse doors begin to open. The wind is so strong that the sting of the air is nearly unbearable on my eyes. A group led by Reverend Thomas slowly walks down the stairs of the courthouse and in our direction. Something immediately feels wrong, and I notice that the group looks smaller than what it was in the morning. Panic hits me as I realize that something terrible has occurred. Perhaps the others gave confessions and were allowed to walk free, yet I am doubtful that such a pleasantry transpired. I notice Ezekiel and Samuel to be the only children in the crowd of officials. We gasp as Ezekiel collapses to the ground. Officials pull Ezekiel to his feet and drag him unsparingly until they reach the prison.

We panic at the sound of the prison doors opening above

our heads. They have returned and we are all eagerly peering from our cells at their arrival. Light shines through our hallway as officials traverse down the stairs and begin to place our friends back in their cell. The officials move quickly and ignore the screams bursting from every cell. Samuel lifts Ezekiel as he tries to protect him on the way back into confinement. They are thrown into the cell, and the officials exit just as quickly as they came. While it be difficult to see from our end of the hallway, the shouting of others indicates that my instincts were honest.

"What happened in there?"

"Did thee confess?"

"Where is everyone else?"

Demands and questions ring through the hall in an attempt to get some answers.

"Silence!" Samuel shouts to regain order in our prison. "I shall tell you all of our torture."

Samuel is visibly in distress from the horrors that he has endured. We anxiously await the words he struggles to reveal.

"They came for us and took us to the courthouse with no explanation," Samuel begins calmly, "and placed us in a disgusting basement, with cells just like these under the courthouse. One by one they took us from the basement for interrogation, and I hid in the corner, so they did not see me. I was too frightened, so I watched as all my friends went voluntarily." Samuel begins to cry as he continues his recollection. "I could hear it all above my head through the floor. Thomas asked them to vividly recall our gathering in the forest on All Hallows Eve. They accused Rose of polluting our minds with witchcraft and training us to take over Warren Hollow with the Devil's assistance. After hours of repetition and influence from Thomas, some of the others began to speak names, throwing accusations for their own safety and acting afflicted. Eventually I decided to make my way from the cell, and I peeked through the small window of the basement door. Our parents lined the stands and watched as our friends stood there helpless. Reverend Thomas told them to confess their sins of witchcraft to God and to beg for his forgiveness. Ezekiel eventually shouted in revolt, prompting Reverend Thomas to approach him. Although they were chained at the hands and ankles, there was some freedom for movement, and Ezekiel attacked the Reverend. He lunged at Thomas and bit him on the neck, causing mass commotion and panic within the courtroom. The others followed Ezekiel and either tried to fight back or escape. Our friends stood no chance and many immediately faced the ultimate punishment of death for doing so."

Samuel struggles to explain himself as we all listen in complete dismay. Although he wishes not to speak another word, his story has not yet reached its end.

"Some were choked with their own chains in front of their parents, while others simply died from the brutality of the brawl. Ezekiel was purposely the only person detained instead of murdered, and then he met a fate worse than death." Samuel places his hand on Ezekiel's shoulder, who fights to remain conscious against the cell bars. "Reverend Thomas instructed his officials to remove Ezekiel's tongue. So that is precisely what occurred right at that instant. Our parents cheered as Ezekiel shouted in pain, and after a few moments they tried to force him back to the basement. I was too frightened to move so they immediately discovered my presence by the door. And rather than punishing me, Reverend Thomas smiled and instructed that we were to be brought back together. 'Tis true that I am a coward." Samuel breaks down in uncontrollable emotion.

I cannot comprehend the tragedy that has occurred within the courthouse. Perhaps our most defiant group of children faced questioning together, and now nearly all of them are dead. Nobody had the chance to properly confess and discover what would come next. Ezekiel could not contain his emotions and decided to take a stand to the Reverend and paid a price in return. Our questions remain unanswered and any signs of reason among our parents or officials has vanished. With certainty this shall change Thomas's plans upon confession or trial, and possibly reassure him of his confidence in execution.

"Such an exaggerated recollection of events, Samuel. Spoken like the true coward you claim thyself to be," an approaching voice mutters.

Silence immediately falls across the prison as Reverend Thomas and the officials make their way down the stairs. He holds his neck in agony, blood dripping down the rest of his body from Ezekiel's attack. He slowly walks through the hall, spending time peering into the cells as he moves forward. One by one Thomas analyzes everyone, studying what months of confinement has done to us. He slows his pace until he comes to a complete stop nearly halfway to Thomasin and I's cell, and I notice he holds a rope in his other hand.

"Too far gone," Thomas begins, "you are all so distant from the light that the opportunity to confess thy sins to God holds no rationality. You pose danger to yourselves, your families, and all of Warren Hollow. Confinement has brought the Devil to the surface and the children that once were have disappeared from your very beings. Your parents witnessed the animals that have become of their children, and all hope of salvation has seemingly vanished." Thomas coughs and struggles to speak while holding his neck. "This winter season shall be the harshest in the colony's history, and it proves unwise to conduct any further trial until the snow melts and the flowers bloom. Perhaps a long winter in these walls shall cleanse and bring confession, and if not, then execution awaits all of you come spring."

No further actions until spring. We cannot last through the winter in these cells and Thomas knows this quite well.

Thomas signals for his officials to unlock Ezekiel's cell. "Bring me the one who assaulted his Reverend. Our business remains unfinished."

After a few moments they begin to aggressively unlock the cell. Ezekiel is barely conscious, yet they show little regard and begin dragging him to Reverend Thomas. We panic at the horror unfolding before us. Samuel tries to fight off the officials and is mercilessly struck over the head. He falls back into the cell, pouring blood and now in agonizing pain.

"Ezekiel Abernathy, I give thee one final attempt to confess thy sins. Tell us of your wrongdoings and we shall see to your forgiveness and set you free at once," Thomas says.

Ezekiel is dropped to his knees and slowly looks up to Thomas. His eyes are barely open and full of tears, blood dripping down his face uncontrollably. Ezekiel attempts to open his mouth but the ability to speak has diminished.

"I cannot hear you child; I give you one final chance to confess. Admit to this treasonous behavior and we shall see that redemption awaits you. Perhaps an apology would suffice as well."

Reverend Thomas removes his hand from his neck and reveals a vicious wound. He winces in pain before regaining his composure and tormenting our friend once more. Thomas humiliates Ezekiel in front of us to convey a message. Like Rose's dramatic execution, this torture of Ezekiel is to instill fear and establish his power. Ezekiel will undoubtedly lose his life in this encounter. I slowly remove myself from the bars of the cell and lay on our mattress facing the wall. I do not wish to see my dearest friend and brother's savior tortured as an example.

Ezekiel has no fight left inside. Just like Rose, death is a welcoming thought that would see the end of such torment. Ezekiel finally opens his mouth, blood pouring from his lips with every attempt to gather words. This would be an impossible task, as Ezekiel's ability to speak another word was taken moments prior. Reverend Thomas laughs at this pathetic attempt.

"Ezekiel of Abernathy descent, I sentence you to death for refusal to comply and valid counts of witchcraft. You broke village ordinance and articulated a ritual in the forest, so for that you must suffer for thy sins."

The others begin to shout and plead for their friend. I lay silently on our mattress, blocking out all sounds and focusing on the beautiful icicles that now form on our cell window just above me.

They grow longer each day as the temperature outside becomes frigid. If one of these icicles were to fall, it could certainly pierce through my skin, hopefully my skull as well, and kill me in this instant. I could move, yet I choose to lay my head under the window day after day, almost hoping for one to fall and set me free. That is one of the less painful ways I could die in this cell. Trials shall not resume until the solstice, which is a death sentence in itself. If it is not self-induced starvation, Reverend Thomas, or the sharpness of such an icicle, I shall lie here and patiently wait for the cold to take me in the night. No longer do I wish to remain faithful. Rather, I simply wish to die.

Reverend Thomas stretches the rope with a smile on his face. Unlike with Rose, Thomas is now taking full pleasure in this moment and forcefully places the rope around Ezekiel's neck himself. Officials assist in restraining Ezekiel and begin dragging him to the stairs. Children shout as they pass by, yet all I can hear is the horrid laughter of the Reverend. They reach the stairs, and after a few moments the commotion is over. Everyone rushes to their cell windows and fights for a view of the outside. In a state of shock, I rise from our mattress and fasten the bucket to view the center of the village. Thomas and his officials come into sight, dragging Ezekiel by the rope on his neck. They pull him like an animal, and Reverend Thomas instructs his officials to place Ezekiel on the platform. The rope is fastened and thrown over the largest branch of the tree. With no hesitation, Reverend Thomas begins to aggressively pull. He pulls with such force that the branch bends, nearly snapping, as Ezekiel now hangs in the air. Clearly defeated and ready for this tragedy to end, Ezekiel shows minimal signs of struggle. Children continue to shout for mercy, while I watch in silence just like before. A few moments pass and the remaining signs of life within Ezekiel vanish from his hanging body. Once more we have witnessed a dear friend's murder.

"Thomasin," I say stoically.

"What is it, Emelie?" She replies through her tears.

"I am going to kill Reverend Thomas."

IX

Fall From Grace

I toss and turn on this poor excuse of a bed, fighting the pain of the cold and failing to ease my mind. Ezekiel's death is a vision I cannot release. He did not deserve such torture, nor did Rose or any of us. If only our parents could see that there is no truth to these matters. They shall never reach such a conclusion now. But to this day, witchcraft is not something that any of us truly understand or practice. We heard the stories of nearby communities, all the outlandish claims of affliction and the executions, never imagining that our village would capitulate to such a force. How can the many educated members of The Hollow fall so blindly into this circumstance?

'Tis hard to continue prayer, as it is of little use. Our words will land on the ears of none, and no higher power shall come to free us from this hell. In honesty, faith has led our entire lives and is the reason we are enslaved. We prayed in the morning, before every meal, and before bed. Then most days were spent in church, reading the bible and confronting our sinful ways in a holy institution. Reverend Nicholas would never have allowed such treatment if he was still alive. He would have protected us, ensuring our parents that these accusations are nothing more than preposterous ideas deserving little recognition. Instead, we are stricken with Thomas, who used this hysteria as an opportunity to assert his dominance. Rose was captured within days of Nicholas's death, as if Thomas was merely waiting for the right opportunity to begin his reign of destruction on Warren Hollow. Thomas held an utter hatred for Rose, prior to any talks of witchcraft. We could never quite understand why, but she was the one he despised worst of all.

Rather than to provide guidance and salvation, Thomas uses religion for willful ignorance. Our parents would never dare to question their faith or the teachings of a Reverend, but unfortunately for them, us children have. All our parents cannot, or perhaps refuse, to see through Thomas's deception. But it is easy for our parents to relinquish control, knowing firsthand that my parents were fearful of my desire for freedom. Like nearly all the other children reaching maturity alongside me, we do not wish for a simple life in this mundane village, destined to become nothing more than a family name until our deaths. They watched as we grew to become individual beings, questioning our destiny and thinking for ourselves. Just like the officials of the court who could not understand or control this witch hysteria, our parents found it justifiable to give Thomas total control.

If I have an issue with washing clothes every morning in the brook, or Thomasin and Samuel engage in intimate behavior, then it is certainly witchcraft. Anything outside of normal behavior and all these awful restrictions in their eyes must be the work of the Devil.

Instead of accepting our desires or allowing freedom, 'tis much easier to throw us into prison like animals waiting for slaughter. Rose was the only person in all of Warren Hollow that understood us, opening our eyes to a world with no limitations. She was always a guiding figure in our lives, but much more so as we began to mature. We would spend hours at her home, complaining of such restrictions and expressing all of our desires. Rose would listen to every word, and provided the respect that we gave to her.

"Thomasin, have you fallen asleep?" I ask quietly.

"I'm afraid not, 'tis freezing in this cell," she replies.

I crawl over Thomasin's bed, pulling myself close to kindle any amount of warmth.

"Do you remember when we would spend the nights at Rose's home?" I ask.

Thomasin laughs at my words, recalling every detail as though it has just occurred. "I cannot believe our parents allowed such behavior. We were but a few years removed from birth, staying awake until the late hours of the night."

"Our parents trusted and respected her. 'Tis my wish to have given her a proper goodbye."

Prior to Rose's capture, Thomasin and I became even closer with her as we approached adulthood. Rather than spending days engaging in games and telling fantasy tales through the night, most children began putting an end to such behaviors. While we still desired our time with Rose, we no longer wished to receive the same treatment as the younger children. And so, our forest bonfires developed. A few years back, Rose organized a lovely fire for the children too old to partake in those same actions anymore. 'Twas nothing more than a small gathering outside of her home on a peaceful night. We sat by the fire and discussed the troubles of our daily lives. This grew in scale to eventually become the massive celebrations that we held until All Hallows Eve. Rose enjoyed our company, and perhaps used this as an opportunity to tame our wild desires. She probably believed that this regular occurrence would allow us the freedom we desired, so that we would not completely disrupt the normality of the village. Regardless of her intentions, we all appreciated her efforts and the opportunity to escape reality. There was no harm in it, as we all had a wonderful time together. 'Twas the farthest situation from Devil worship or ritualistic behavior.

And to the surprise of none, the capture of our idol pushed us into this state of revolt.

"Rose was only a few years beyond our age now when she came to The Hollow," Thomasin begins. "She knew it better than anyone, we would not accept this life for what it was."

"She understood us, because she shared a similar burning within herself. She knew that this village was not the place for such behavior, which is why I believe she held all those bonfires. 'Tis true that she wanted to have joy in our company, but maybe she knew what would happen if we did not have a way to express that freedom," I say.

While I begin thinking my thoughts aloud, there is not a person who could understand me better than Thomasin. We have known each other since our birth, and often tell each other secrets that we wouldn't dare reveal to anyone else.

"Perhaps she missed our company, and wanted a way to keep a relationship as we grew older. Rose put herself at risk for us," Thomasin replies.

"I do wish I could have one final conversation with her, thanking her for all that she has done for us. From healing my brother to teaching us all that we know."

We talk through the night of tales from our childhood, reminiscing and reliving those wonderful memories. Joyful conversation helps to keep the focus from the cold and harshness of our situation.

The sunshine through our window indicates the start to another day, but the light brings no change to the temperature. We freeze through the nights, and now through the days as well. These

frigid conditions are enough to drive anyone mad. Yet I attempt to remain calm, spending the days formulating a plot to end Thomas's life. I truly meant those words as I spoke them to Thomasin. Reverend Thomas deserves a fate worse than Rose or Ezekiel. 'Tis he who should be locked in a cell through the winter.

We cannot understand how our parents, other members of the church, and even the officials of the court can stand by while such unjust behavior unfolds. They have relinquished total control to Thomas, and his viciousness knows no bounds. Perhaps Rose could have survived if she confessed, or our friends would still be alive if they cooperated in the court. It will never be known for certain, and now a similar fate awaits us come spring. With the dead of winter drawing near, I fear that there shall be none of us left to witness the conclusion to this catastrophe.

Will someone come to save us, swiping the power from Thomas and breaking the locks to our cells? Surely the other communities shall take notice of the horrors unfolding in Warren Hollow. Is it not the most vital farming community in all of New England as they say? How long can this torture possibly go on? Days, weeks, years?

My thoughts could overtake me if I spend too much time lost in my mind. Hours spent reaching the point of near insanity occurs daily, obsessing over the possible outcomes and envisioning a perfect ending to this nightmare. But the others have begun looking to me for guidance, so preparation for all outcomes is necessary for success.

Regardless of our own struggles and fears, the others have taken care of each other to the best of their ability. We all share food, quilts, and converse so that nobody feels alone. 'Tis necessary to remain as one if we wish to survive. I attempt to hide my own struggles from the others, and perhaps Thomasin is the only one who can see right through it. She knows me too well to think I am not affected or intentionally harming myself. Some nights she will try to comfort me and dive into this guilt that I face, but I remain distant, even from my dearest friend. This is a struggle I do not wish for her to truly understand.

Such endless guilt. Blaming myself for all of this, worrying night and day about my brother. I simply cannot bear it. But how could I ever tell my friend that I wish to die?

These dark thoughts never entered my mind prior to our conviction. I have always seen myself as a peaceful being, caring for people, animals, and nature. Warren Hollow has endured its share of violence throughout my life, something that I have intentionally kept a great distance from. But times are different, and we must act before Thomas kills all of us. We cannot wait for a savior or hope that a fair trial shall continue in the spring. Thomas said it himself, we will die upon spring's arrival, and there not be a force that will stop him.

God, if you still listen to my words, please forgive me for these wicked thoughts. For I do not see any other way out of this mess. Please, give me the chance to face the Reverend.

Just as the sun beamed in the sky and shined through our window, the light begins to fade. Any indication of darkness halts all contemplation and progress on our plans throughout the day. Some of the others continue with prayer, begging for the power to make it through such harsh conditions. The night is not the time for revenge, as all focus must land on staying close to one another and surviving.

Each day is none but the same. The days become shorter and the temperature colder. The others will ask of my thoughts, hoping I have found a solution to get us out of such a mess. Some days are more successful than others, although all track of time becomes a blur of light and darkness. Thomasin and I have explained a precise path to Rose's home from the prison, indicating that anyone fortunate enough to escape shall venture there. While we have a plan to act upon once we are out of the prison, 'tis breaking free from the prison that be the issue.

"Night draws near once more," I shout down the hall, "perhaps it be best to stop for the day and prepare for the darkness."

On my command, the others begin to halt all progress on planning and any means of escape. I find it easiest to announce the night as it draws near, something the others have asked of me over the past few days. Still, I struggle to hold such a newfound level of respect and power. Questions are presented to me as if I know all of the answers, and every thought is verified with me prior to any actions. Oftentimes I do feel strange giving direction or becoming the leader. Some of the others cannot think rationally or remain calm, so they often look to me for all forms of guidance. Ever since my cooperation in the church, it's as though I am but a newly appointed leader with wisdom above the others. But I am simply me, the same person who wished for no attention and would often escape to nature to avoid such recognition. 'Tis an unexpected occurrence that baffles me at times, yet I hold such regard with high importance. If there is any possibility to free us from these bars, then I shall certainly do so.

Sure enough the others prepare to rest for the night, thanking me for devising plans and all of my efforts. While they attempt to find peace and warmth through the night, I have no intentions of doing so. I cannot rest until John is back in my arms and we are a great distance from this forsaken place. With my back to the frozen wall of our cell, I shall sit lost in my mind until the sun rises once more.

> *Escape...*
>
> *Find John...*
>
> *Kill Thomas...*
>
> *Escape...*
>
> *Find John...*
>
> *Kill Thomas...*

But how? There *must* be a way, you cannot rest until you find a way. The others depend on your success, and you must save thy brother.

> *Escape...*
>
> *Find John...*
>
> *Kill Thomas...*
>
> *Escape...*
>
> *Find John...*
>
> *Kill Thomas...*

x

When Death Comes Knocking

Massive snowfall has hit The Hollow, with the strongest blizzard of my lifetime strengthening day after day. The icicles on our window have reached sword length, and a full layer of ice now blocks our view to the outside. However, this is positive because a barrier between our cell and the incredible snowfall now exists. The weather has become unbearable to the highest extent. Most children go days without communication or any movements, for the air is too frigid to move but a muscle. Officials bring us food, often once every few days now, but it is typically frozen or spoiled upon its arrival. Thomasin and I continue to whisper through the night as we lay side by side, and without her I would undoubtedly succumb to such torture.

A few of the younger children near the stairs were not as fortunate, as the blistering conditions have ended their lives. The officials will simply remove the bodies of anyone deceased when they bring us our meals. Death has grown quite near for me on some of those nights, yet I somehow survive and remain on this earth, trapped in this cell. Perhaps the care of my friend, or my determination to save John, keeps me living through this hell that we endure. Life stands still behind these walls, as the only balance of time is light and darkness. The distinction between days, weeks, or months has become impossible to comprehend. Ezekiel's execution could have happened a few days ago or a few months ago; I remember it all the same as it is lost in time.

I sit in conception, nearly going mad while I devise a way to successfully kill Reverend Thomas and make an escape. Regardless of any plots or new ideas, all outcomes lead to my own death. However, like Rose and Ezekiel, I feel that this would be a mercy. If Thomas is killed then his leadership will end, allowing another leader to return order to our village. Death brought Thomas to The Hollow, so death shall bring another Reverend who may save us. Other children would want nothing more than to end Reverend Thomas's reign with their own hands, but I could not ask anyone to make such a sacrifice. There has not been a single visit from Reverend Thomas since the day he murdered Ezekiel, so I fear that the chance may never present itself. Word has spread successfully of our immaculate escape across all cells, so the plan remains the same. Any child who can free themself shall assist in freeing others and venture to Rose's home in the forest. We will regroup there and devise a strategy to travel as far away as possible.

During these harsher days we all sit in silence, but when the temperatures rise, we quickly try everything possible to create makeshift weapons from stones and the other few contents of our cells. Sharp objects that resemble knives have been passed down the hall, and some children work tirelessly on loosening their bars or breaking free from the few windows. William and Robert have begun to carve around the edges of their cell door, and significant progress has been made. They may be the ones who actually break free of their cell and free us all. Thomasin and I have made efforts to loosen the bars on the windows, but 'tis of no use. Until the snow halts and the ice melts, the window provides just as much escape as the solid walls before us. Aside from the window, we also work day and night to break the lock to our cell, reaching our hands through the bars and using the tools to try and release the lock's tension.

This determination across our group keeps us alive each day, as the possibility of freedom is closer than ever before. As word of where to go travels through the prison, I continue to receive praise and acknowledgement from everyone. All my time spent fixating on our escape has provided enough hope to the others for a chance of survival. My knowledge of the forest is recognized so they listen closely to my every word. Most people in Warren Hollow have never seen Rose's home deep in the forest, but I have spent many days there and know its precise location. Further discussion of how to find and free the younger children is also of concern. I worry day and night for John's survival, and reaching those children shall prove as extremely difficult. But our younger brothers and sisters deserve freedom as well, so we must take them with us on our journey. Some of those poor children are no more than a few years removed from birth.

I have decided that no matter how irrational or dangerous the plan, I shall be the one to free John and the rest of the children.

"I need to find him, Thomasin. I shall fight my way into their confinement and free the children who have survived this long," I say.

"Then it is settled, Emelie," Thomasin begins, "I will assist you while the others venture to Rose's house. You cannot take such action alone, and together we will have a better chance of saving them."

"I want to do this alone, Thomasin. It's dangerous and you should not risk your freedom. And the others mustn't know of my plan to kill Thomas, it will cause chaos and shift the focus to violence."

"You are my dearest friend; you have kept me alive in this cell and have provided a prison full of our friends the hope of freedom. It would be an honor to assist you once we find a way out, and I shall not speak a word of your deeper plans to anyone. But I must go with you."

I realize that she will not easily change her mind. We debate for a few moments until I finally agree to her assistance. Thomasin is a good friend, and she wants to fill her role and find a purpose in this madness.

The plans have finally come together, and our escape draws near. We are potentially hours removed from someone finally breaking through their lock. As soon as this occurs, we will set our escape in motion. I shall be of the first released from the cells and immediately begin our rescue mission. The others will assist in breaking locks and chains until everyone is freed, all while Thomasin and I stealthily rescue the younger children. Then we will all make our way from The Hollow to Rose's home in the forest.

Ambitious thoughts racing through my mind are interrupted by warnings from the other children. Someone approaches from the stairs, so we immediately halt all progress and conceal our tools. I toss my makeshift blade below my pillow and sit on top of it obediently. Footsteps slowly come down the stairs and stop at the end of the hallway. Our progress is highly noticeable while looking around at the neighboring cells, so I pray that it is of little attention to whoever approaches.

We have come too far for our plan to fall apart. Please do not let them notice. Not when we are so very close.

"Listen carefully," a voice says.

I now realize it is Reverend Thomas who joins us in our prison. "I am looking for Emelie. Emelie Williams. Make thy presence known."

My heart stops and I sit frozen on our mattress. What could Thomas desire with me? We have not seen anyone since Ezekiel's death, so why does he come for me?

Tis time for your execution. The day has come for you to be made an example, just like Rose and Ezekiel. He must have crept into the prison and listened from above while you became the appointed leader. So now you must face punishment.

"Emelie!" Thomas shouts with growing impatience, "Make thy presence known at once!"

"Here, Reverend," the words faintly escape my mouth. I feel as though another force is in control of my body, making me rise from the mattress and guiding my way to the cell bars. My arm stretches into the hallway to alert Reverend Thomas of my location. He slowly walks over and stares through the cell bars. For the first time I come face to face with evil. We stare at each other for a few moments, never once breaking my gaze into his eyes. I immediately notice the scar on his neck from Ezekiel's attack. Perhaps he waits for me to cower or back down. Instead, I match his intensity and look directly through him, showing no emotion.

"Step away from the bars and over to the wall," Thomas orders us. We place our backs to the wall under the window, the cold burns against my skin upon contact. To my surprise, I recognize that Thomas is alone. He does not have a force of officials behind him, so confusion begins to fall over me. Thomas unlocks our cell, making his way into our area and now standing directly before us.

Thomasin begins to panic at his presence and nervously pleads to him.

"What will you do to us?"

Thomas turns his attention to her, and I sense his growing anger. "This does not concern you, for you will obey and pay us no mind!" Thomas pushes her to the ground forcefully, she cries out as she lands next to our mattress. Thomasin defeatedly crawls over to the pillow that conceals our weapons. Her hand furtively reaches under, and she meets my gaze. However, with little movement I signal for her to pause her attack. Curiosity strikes me and I try to uncover Reverend Thomas's intentions.

"What do you want with me, Reverend?" I ask sternly, attempting to show no fear. If Thomas desired an execution, then he would have taken a different approach. "I need you to come at once. Any attempt to flee and you shall die. For this is of urgency," Thomas says, offering no further reasoning.

I do not understand. He must have discovered our plans. Perhaps my spirit slipped away and attacked someone in their dreams, as we have been accused of.

Reverend Thomas places chains around my hands and leads me out of the cell. We make our way out into the walkway, and I analyze each cell as we pass. My friends watch on as I slowly pass them one by one. Rather than shouting and pleading like in prior situations, the others watch in complete silence. They stare motionless as I walk by, perhaps fearful that my plans and ambitions shall die on this day. I now stand at the bottom of the stairs, Thomas pushing me from behind for further movement. I begin to climb the stairs, quickly noticing how weak my legs have become. Months of sitting frozen in our cell and the conditions we face have weakened my body. Each step comes with struggle and pain, yet I eventually reach the top and await further instruction from Thomas. He moves past me to unlock the main prison doors. Before we make an exit, Thomas provides me with shoes and a coat.

"Put on these coverings for now, but you will not be permitted to keep anything upon our return," Thomas instructs.

My return? I will return to the prison? Perhaps this is not my execution.

Thomas pushes the doors open, and I am blinded by the blistering light of the sun. Heavy snowfall pours and I notice that our village is covered from the ongoing storm. We are officially in the heart of winter. "Now, you are to follow behind me and do not try anything of suspicion."

"Where are we going, Reverend?" I ask impatiently. Anger visibly grows in Thomas, but he remains calm and grabs my chain to guide me. We make our way down the prison stairs, and I raise my arm to block the heavy winds and snowfall that we face. Descending the stairs further proves to be a challenge, and my arms are so weakened that I cannot keep them raised for long. I follow in the footsteps of Thomas, watching his legs rather than the path ahead of us. The winds are far too strong to stare ahead. I notice that we are not moving towards the courthouse or the center of town. We take a different route, perhaps to the church.

Surprisingly, we pass the turn to the church, and I am puzzled as to where we are traveling. I catch glimpses of houses through the blizzard as we continue forward. Snowfall rises nearly to my knees as we progress, adding further difficulty to every individual step. We walk silently until I begin recognizing our surroundings. This section of The Hollow is where my home is, as the route we follow is precisely my path back home after chores. All forest retreats conclude with walking this path, as I always analyze the houses and families on my way by.

It was months ago that I witnessed a mother scold her child over a pumpkin in that very spot. 'Tis my hope that he is still alive with the others.

There be no main village structures back this way, only

homes and the other gate to leave The Hollow. The distance to my home grows shorter and thoughts of fear finally rise inside me. I have not pondered on Mother and Father in weeks, and I certainly cannot bear the sight of our home at this point. We make another turn, which would lead directly to us passing my home. Tears begin to form at the thoughts in my mind. The last time I walked this path was on All Hallows Eve, with John on my back. Now I follow the same route in chains, nearly frozen to death and under the will of the person who ruined my life. However, this walk has allowed me to uncover possible exit strategies and further plan for an escape. The snow is much thicker on this side of The Hollow, yet we would go completely unnoticed. My initial plan was to exit the village closer to the prison, but I know this path much better and now see that we could escape unfollowed. Most homes are boarded up to prevent the weather from entering doors and windows, or possibly to ward off witches and keep the evil outside.

We grow closer to my home, so I keep my eyes to the ground. I wish not to see any glimpse, so I return to watching only Reverend Thomas's steps directly in front of me. I know we are but seconds from passing by, so I hold my breath and try to calm myself. Thomas suddenly comes to a complete stop.

I raise my view, and in a state of shock I stand directly in front of my home. Thomas turns to face me and glares into my eyes without speaking a word. He recognizes the fear and panic that I now fail to conceal and offers a grin at the sight of my distress. Perhaps he was surprised at my will in the prison and offered some respect in turn, but just like the others, he thrives off the fact that I too have been broken.

"We have arrived, child. Shall we go inside?"

XI

Savior

O vercome by absolute terror, I prepare to enter the home that has since been banished from my mind. Rather than acting quickly or trying to run, my mind empties of all thoughts, and I am no longer in control. My body floats forward, and I simply wish to be anywhere else in the world. Within my head, I am but frolicking through the forest on a warm summer's day, away from the snowfall and fatigue of my being. Unfortunately, I realize no desires or thoughts shall rescue me from whatever torment lies ahead. My heart begins to beat uncontrollably, reminding me that I am still alive and capable of feeling the emotions that I have suppressed. I reach the stairs to my home and spot a path through the heavy snowfall that is evenly plowed. With hesitation I climb the stairs until we are directly in line with the door.

This is the door I have thoughtlessly passed through thousands of times in my life. Sometimes after chores, or even in the late hours of the night after escaping. What awaits on the other side? Pure shock has prevented me from solving this puzzling situation. Perhaps I am still dreaming. Maybe I slowly die in my cell at this moment, with my life flashing before my eyes. I am certain death would be more pleasant than whatever awaits through this threshold.

Reverend Thomas pushes past me and knocks on the door. We stand in silence, and I notice Thomas directing a few menacing glances my way. Pretending not to notice his glare, I nervously stare directly to the ground before me. Shuffling on the other side indicates that someone is greeting our arrival. The door opens and I keep my gaze to the ground. Slowly I begin to look, realizing that I stand no more than a single step from Father. We stare at each other for what feels like hours on end. He appears unrecognizable, though I am certain he feels the same for my appearance. Father looks to be a shadow of the man I knew months ago, the unraveling of events in Warren Hollow has certainly impacted him as well. His hair hangs long and unkept, and for the first time in memory he has grown a beard, rendering him nearly a stranger.

"Father."

The only word I can speak at the moment. I feared for the anger or sadness that would occur passing our home, let alone the sight of Mother or Father, yet in this moment I feel nothing. Emotions of positivity or negativity remain concealed, as I stand here in dismay. Father begins to open his mouth while analyzing my appearance. He raises his hand to emphasize his words, yet no words ever escape. After a few moments trapped in an unbreakable stare, Father steps aside and signals for our entry.

I take a few steps until I stand inside, nervously brushing the snow from my clothes and hair. Warmth from our fireplace greets our arrival, and I fearfully look around our home. The few decorations we had in place are no longer present, and the overall atmosphere is depressing and dark. Our home looks as though it has been left vacant, as all the joy and care was destroyed months ago. I nearly forget my current situation and think to make myself comfortable. On a normal day I would rush inside to greet Mother and Father, then assist my brother in playtime or preparations for dinner. Now, I stand in chains as a prisoner, understanding that this shall never be my home again.

"Sit, Emelie, for we have an unpleasantry to handle,"

Reverend Thomas says while directing me to my favorite chair by the window. He sits me down and removes the chains that bind me. His gentle tone is merely a ploy to prevent Mother and Father from discovering his wickedness. "You shall obey all commands and do not speak out of question. Full cooperation and validation of claims may begin the process of redemption and freedom. Thy Mother and Father would like to discuss recent circumstances which have brought you to this very situation today."

"Freedom? Is this part of my trial?" I ask with confusion. Thomas takes a step closer to my chair. "That will not be necessary, Emelie. With cooperation, we shall go through the procedures and validate the claims from thy brother."

"John? Where is my brother? Of what claims do you speak?" I begin to raise my voice. I jump to my feet and this commotion draws Mother to enter the room. She lays eyes on me and stops in her tracks. Tears form in her eyes, and she begins to force a smile at my presence.

"Emelie, my daughter. What a fine day before us," Mother says unnervingly. I study her features and movements as she begins to greet me. Mother looks worse than Father, as though she has spent the passing months in prison as well. Although she speaks happily and in a caring manner, I know that the Mother of my memory is not the woman before me today. All the beauty has vanished from her appearance, making her nearly unrecognizable as well.

Who are these strange people in my home? Nothing but mere ghosts of the Mother and Father I once knew.

This home is not the same place that it was prior to All Hallows Eve. The atmosphere feels evil and deceptive, as though something terrible is bound to occur.

"Now my sweet daughter, we have much to discuss," Mother begins calmly, "your brother, John, has fallen quite ill as of recent. We fear his time on this earth has reached its end. But do not fear, for he has given us the truth. John has informed us of his influence on you and the other children. We know he spoke to the Devil and acted to honor his sinful ways and open himself to pure evil. We shall forgive you for any wrongdoings under his influence. You can speak the truth, Emelie, the Devil will no longer lead you through thy brother. Then you shall find redemption."

I stare blankly at Mother for a few moments in complete horror. "John is ill?" I ask before breaking hysterically into tears. I fall to the chair and hide my face from everyone in the room. In no manner can I comprehend the information that Mother calmly provided me.

This cannot be the end. I am going to save John and free the others before we regroup at Rose's home. We are going to embark on a journey to another village far away. Saving John is my purpose.

"Do not fear, Emelie, for John has confessed of his sins and shall receive his final judgment. 'Tis not us who holds such power, for it is God who decides. You know this," Mother reassures me. She speaks with intent as if the child she cared deeply for is but a dog. I knew that something was wrong from the moment Reverend Thomas lifted me from my cell. My execution holds preference over this current situation. Mother and Father stand at such a distance from reality that a false confession from my brother holds more meaning than his death. Mother grabs my hand and draws herself closer. "Now, John has one request in the instance of his confession. He agreed to provide us with the truth in its entirety, so long as he could see you on this day. John awaits your presence upstairs. The time grows short, for you must validate his claims at once," Mother tells me.

Reverend Thomas assists me in standing from the chair. I get back to my feet and begin to exit the room as Mother and Father anxiously watch my every step. They do not follow as I reach the bottom of the stairs. I'm simply frozen in fear, so I stand in place for what feels like eternity. The realization finally hits me that this shall be the last time I see John. All the plans of freeing the children and escaping to a faraway village will die on this day. Without John, I have no desire to live or carry on with my plans. He was the only force that gave me the will to escape and save the others. If I cannot save my brother, then saving a prison full of my friends is of impossibility.

I feel a hand on my back that gives me a push to begin my ascent. I turn and realize that Reverend Thomas stands by me with a smile. "Go child," Thomas says loudly for Mother and Father to hear. He then leans closer to whisper in my ear. "Watch your heathen brother perish so we can get back to the cells. You shall reunite in hell come spring."

Rather than fighting back, I remain emotionless and simply obey his words. Perhaps it is the shock of this situation or my will to survive fleeting, but I simply follow his command and begin to climb the stairs. I do not draw out my steps at this moment, for John awaits my arrival, so I give it all of my energy and race up to the top. This floor of our home was always the area I occupied much more than anywhere else. John and I would spend hours engaged in play through the hall or in our designated areas, as we created our own fantasy through imagination in this boring structure. I stare at the window of which we made our escape months ago, and immediately feel a sadness overcoming me. Everything from the moment I decided to escape through the window on All Hallows Eve until now has unfolded because of my own selfish choices. But rather than feeling anger towards myself, as I have done every passing day in my cell, I make my way to John. I take one final pause before entering the room to compose myself. My hand shakes as I nervously raise it to turn the handle. Saving myself from this torture for one final moment, I choose to knock at the door before entering. As expected, there is no response, and I realize that I cannot delay my entrance any longer.

"John, can you hear me?" I slowly enter the room and darkness surrounds me. The only light in John's area is a burning candle near the bed. I make my way to the mattress, gently sitting on the corner and I finally focus my gaze on him. He lies motionless on the bed, clinging to life as if it will vanish at any moment. My condition is no match for the state that John is in today, covered in bruises and nearly half his weight. John struggles desperately with every breath. Given his appearance, I notice his health has taken a significant decline and it finally hits me that John lies but moments from his end. Tears begin to pour from my eyes, and I cannot find words, so I simply grab John and pull him into my lap. John slowly awakens as I cradle him in my arms. His expression fills with the last of his excitement upon noticing my presence.

"Sister," John states in a pained struggle, "how I have missed you so."

"And I have missed you John, not a day goes by where I have not given thought to escaping and rescuing you," I reply.

"They told us the stories of Rose and Ezekiel; he saved my life on that day." John coughs and fights for air as he continues. "They would not feed us and made us sleep on the floor. It was too cold in the night; I fear the others are all dead. But I couldn't die, I knew I had to save you."

"No John," I start to cry, "I was to save you. This was all my fault; I should have left you at home and only I would have faced this punishment. You did not deserve any of it and I am truly sorry."

"Do not be sorry, sister, that was the greatest day of my life. Oh how I love the forest."

"What has Reverend Thomas done to you, John? For what did you make confession?" I begin asking John in order to uncover the larger schemes. Reverend Thomas fooled my parents into following along, yet I know that I will never see freedom. I will return to the prison and rot for the rest of winter. And once the spring arrives, we shall face formal execution one by one.

"Thomas would visit and ask us nicely to confess. He said everyone could go home if the bad person confessed, he even promised. I knew I could trick him into freeing you. And it worked, you are here today and he thinks it was me," John says with serious intent. He told Reverend Thomas exactly what he thought would be needed to gain my freedom.

"I did it, sister. Thomas believed my tales, so they will let us free today," John tells me excitedly.

They will never let us go John; Thomas simply wants to torture me in the most horrid way possible. He has used you to pry hope from my soul. But this is a truth that John shall never know.

Rather than telling John the truth, I use all my power to force a smile. His final moments draw near so I hold him tighter and reassure his actions. "Yes John, because of you we shall be free to return to the forest and live the life of our dreams. Thank you, dear brother."

"Yes," John says as he pulls on my sleeve, "we did it."

Johns starts to cough viciously as his breathing slows. He

violently fights himself in my arms, so I carefully place him back into his bed.

"You have saved me," I tell him happily. "Now we are home and must prepare so we can take our grandest adventure once the snow clears," I tearfully instruct.

"Tell me, sister. Where shall we go this time?"

I lie next to him on the bed, my presence bringing him comfort and easing his struggling breath. I pull him closer and gently place his hand in mine.

"Oh John, we shall travel to a faraway village. One where children do not partake in chores or prayer if they do not choose so. A place where we can celebrate All Hallows Eve and decorate every home with pumpkins and flowers. We will spend our days racing through the trees and joking with friends until we grow tired and return home. Then we shall spend the next day doing but the same. This village will be deep in the forest, where the wind sings through the trees and the paths are covered in falling leaves. And we will not escape through a window, we shall pridefully march out of our door to greet the crowd of friends that awaits us outside. For it will be a magical place where we shall honor Rose and Ezekiel and all of those who made such a life possible," I explain.

The tension begins escaping from his grip. Gently I lay John's hand at his side and lower my voice to a whisper. "But most importantly we shall honor you, John. Oh how I love you dear brother."

In this moment, I recognize that his life has escaped, and he peacefully lays at my side, free from struggle and pain. I begin to cry hysterically, pulling John into my arms for one final embrace.

"Oh John, I am so very sorry."

'Tis impossible to find further words. This is not the outcome of which I envisioned. I have failed to save my brother and all of the other children shall die as well.

"You saved me John; you can rest now."

I slowly release my hold and place John back into his bed. Anger fills my body as bitter hatred towards Mother and Father swells. I sat in my cell for months, pondering how they felt about their children in confinement. Hope that they would break free from Reverend Thomas's teachings and rescue us held no value. Mother and Father were never devising a rescue, instead, they followed along and happily welcomed our death as reasonable. John's illness has taken him to the grave, yet Mother and Father only desired a confession to witchcraft beforehand. Mother always cared for John night and day, taking him to Rose's home and assisting his every motion. Until the start of these horrific trials, Mother and Father loved us and paid no mind to outside occurrences. It's as if Mother and Father are different people, the loving parents of months past are dead as well. Regardless of their intentions, I do have gratuity that it was I who held John in his final moments. Nobody ever understood the relationship between us. While Mother and Father provided care, I gave John a life of excitement and allowed him to feel normal among his illnesses. So I fought to stay alive every day in confinement, even when I wished to die myself, in order to rescue John. The fantasy of rescuing him and escaping to a magical village on the other side of the world has also died in this room. He was my brother, and I failed to execute the plan we have developed for months.

Rather than plummeting any further into anger and sadness, I decide it is time to say goodbye and exit the room. I slowly rise to my feet and tuck John into his bed. The quilt pulled right up to his chin as he always demanded. Before leaving I speak one final promise. "I will make it there, John. Your sacrifice shall not be for nothing. Today is the day I make an escape, and I will do it because of you. That I promise."

I want nothing more than to give up and succumb to the inevitable death that awaits. Failure to rescue John has taken any desire to live from my being. However, John's sacrifice cannot go unanswered, so I must escape or die in my attempt. My friends do not deserve to have their freedom stripped because of my own failing will. Lashing out or trying to make my own escape from this room would ultimately lead to my death, so I need to suppress all emotions to safely return to the prison.

I take a long and interrupted gaze at John in his bed, acknowledging that this is the final moment we shall be together. All our memories and plans for the future vanish as I shut the door behind me. I make my way through the hall and pass by the window we climbed through months ago. A bit of sadness overwhelms me at the realization that I will never walk through this home again after today. Yet, I remain unfazed at these thoughts, as a home without my brother is not somewhere I wish to return. Mother and Father are dead as well, for I shall never see them again. And now, the time to face Reverend Thomas has come once more.

Making my way down the stairs, I notice that Mother, Father, and Reverend Thomas eagerly await.

"John has passed," I inform the group as I continue my descent. Mother remains unbothered, yet I notice Father immediately exits to the other room. Perhaps there is some rational thought left in Father, yet he let his son die and watches as his daughter struggles to survive this endless torture.

"Emelie, did thy speak with John?" Mother asks

enthusiastically. "Did he provide you the truth as he hath done with us?"

Rather than lunging to attack Mother where she stands, I simply agree with her remarks. "Yes, Mother, he lifted all evil and now I beg for my forgiveness in this moment," I say.

"So, you confess to all wrongdoings brought on under your brother's influence?"

"Aye, I held no power over myself in those times. Now I feel free, willing to confess my sins as well. I beg thee for forgiveness and seek redemption." I turn to Reverend Thomas and drop to my knees. Tears fall to fully emphasize my confession.

Mother rushes to my side and provides me with comfort. "She confesses, Thomas, you must help to redeem her soul," Mother tells Thomas.

"Rise child. For this is only the beginning," Thomas says.

I stand on my feet and immediately give Mother a meaningless hug to comply. My performance was believable enough for Mother, yet I know Thomas puts on a performance of his own. He shall never give any of us freedom. But if I want to leave our house unharmed, I must act as though I am the witch they fear, but eager to seek redemption. It pains me to label my brother as evil and corrupt, yet he knew this was the only path to freedom for me so I must follow it as well.

"Emelie, you must return to the prison and await your final judgment. We have all witnessed your first step of redemption today, and soon you shall return to us with a cleansed soul. Will you obey and do whatever necessary to achieve forgiveness?" Mother asks.

"Of course, Mother, I shall beg for God's mercy and vigorously await any proceedings that lead to salvation."

"Very well, Emelie. Then you must follow your Reverend. If you fully comply then you shall be released in the near future."

Showing no additional care, Mother begins to climb the stairs. I now stand alone with Reverend Thomas; he smiles at me and starts to fasten my chains once more. We make our way to the main door, and I take a quick glance around our home. Plenty of memories rush through my mind, yet I have no desire to ever return. As we leave, I notice Father peering from the window. He maintains his stare until we turn and are out of eyesight.

Goodbye Mother and Father, I shall never forgive you. Though I will miss the life that once was. You could have saved John, or even prevented my return to the prison that awaits, yet you did nothing. Perhaps you think these actions are justified, yet you have all lost clarity.

To satisfy my brother's final wish, I must place all focus on making my escape. If I am taken back to my cell, then I shall never be free. 'Tis only a matter of time before our weapons and progress are discovered, if not so already. There must be some way I can make an escape on our trip back to the prison. The blizzard rages even more aggressively at this hour. Paths and trails are indistinguishable through the snow, and it seems that Thomas has lost all sense of direction.

Perhaps you can lose Reverend in the snow, or you can wait for the perfect moment and attack him. No, that shall never work. You can barely walk and have no strength to initiate an attack. You must think wise and tactical, something that would raise little suspicion. You need to break free and have enough time to save the others, but how? Think…think…think!

Following Reverend Thomas, thoughts of an escape race through my mind. Feelings of desperation fill my body as I now begin to panic. I cannot run out of time, today may be my only chance to make a move. If Thomas locks me in my cell, then the next time I leave will be for an execution, if the cold does not take me first.

To my surprise, the blizzard's chill does not bother me. Perhaps I run on adrenaline, or the shock from what I witnessed moments ago holds my body in a state of numbness. However, I notice Thomas struggles with the weather as we move forward. He looks side to side, most likely determining a location to take shelter from the storm. The snow falls at a vigorous rate, and winds nearly blow us to the ground. Even I cannot determine our distance from the prison through the wintry conditions. Thomas grabs me aggressively, slamming me into the wall of the farming structure we are currently passing. The force knocks me to the ground, icicles falling all around and nearly piercing my skin. I watch as they hit the ground and shatter into pieces.

"Now child, you must do as I say, or I shall kill you in this instant. We are to wait by this shed until the blizzard clears, then we will return to the prison. If you try to escape, I will not wait until the spring. I will strangle you and leave you to freeze in the snow. Doth thou understand?" Thomas aggressively instructs. I do not answer in a timely fashion, so Thomas rips the coat from my body and strikes me across the face.

Out of nowhere, everything slows to full stillness in my body. Total clarity washes through my mind, and I feel as though I am but an onlooker watching us from afar. Any thoughts that rushed through my head have halted as well. I live in this moment, knowing that whatever actions I choose will determine the outcome of the rest of my life. Today I will escape or die trying, but no emotions overcome me, nor do I fear a failed attempt at escape. I know that my promise to John must be fulfilled, so success is completely necessary. In my mind, every detail of the torture I have endured plays out thoroughly. Escaping from the window, the attack in the forest, months of starvation, nearly freezing to death in a cell, watching icicles grow longer by the day above my head with the hope that they fall, Rose and Ezekiel's brutal deaths, and John passing in my arms. Replaying these events leads me to a pivotal discovery.

It suddenly hits me with as much force as the attack on All Hallows Eve. The perfect escape plan has fallen into my mind. There is one way to escape this situation and save the others. Everything must unravel precisely according to my vision, for I shall die if the slightest mishap occurs. With my life on the line, I know it is time to set the plan in motion.

For John.

XII

Desperate Measures

My escape was secured the moment that Reverend Thomas opened the cell door and marched me to my former home. Whether I exit into the forest or into the afterlife, I shall not return to that cell as a prisoner. The plan in my mind is one of danger and risk, yet I must prevail for the freedom of the others. A prison full of friends awaits my return, and my guidance has provided them the hope to survive each day. Endless nights spent creating weapons and building upon my own plans must hold significance. If I am to die then so it shall be, but my friends must achieve freedom from confinement prior to my demise. Nobody else will receive the opportunity of which I was granted today, and this be Thomas's mistake. He paid no mind to John's words, only retrieving me from the prison to make another example of someone.

And that mistake shall cost him his life.

The plan in my head is but one of deceit and betrayal, yet the results shall bring honor to my decisions. I may put the others at risk, as well as myself, through the actions I will set in motion momentarily.

"Tell me, child," Thomas asks menacingly, "did you feel sadness watching your brother draw his final breaths? He held on as long as he could, even after days without food. And in his final moments he thought he could use deceit to free you. Yet no servant of Satan shall ever walk free from the prison walls. That is until the arrival of spring, and we can proceed with digging holes, fit for witches and sinners."

Do not attack him. Think of thy friends, if the plan is to work then you must remain composed, for he has no idea what awaits.

"Aye feel nothing, Reverend. My brother carried sin, adopted from Rose the apothecary. He influenced my every move. With John at rest, I seek to redeem my soul and return to Mother and Father," I tell Thomas.

"Save thy lies, child. Do not play tricks on thee, your brother spoke a convincing tale. Yet I know it was one of desperation and heroics. You will not do the same. We must make way for that cell so you can rot your days away. But first we must gather my men at the church for a proper inspection. I hear whispers of an escape forming, so we shall check every one of you heathens for treachery." Thomas begins to pull me upwards so we can continue braving the blizzard.

"Wait!" I yell desperately and rip myself from his grasp.

Time to set my escape in motion.

"Reverend, thy cannot make me go back to that cell. Place me anywhere else, leave me outside if you must. I simply cannot return to the evil within my cell," I tell Thomas in a panicked exaggeration.

"Of what evil doth thou speak?"

"I do not think I can fully speak it, Reverend, for she will know I exposed the plans and murder me upon return."

"Who?"

"The one I share a cell with, Thomasin Roberts. She be the most evil of all. She whispers to the Devil and dances naked in the moon's light, plotting to murder the others as an offering to the

Devil. She even cuts me for my blood and curses me. Weapons are hidden in our cell, and she will use them to make an escape at any moment. Tis she, the rest of us will make no effort to disobey our redemption," I begin to cry. Thomas stares at me closely, unsure of how to react. "Thou shall not fool me child. Speak of the truth or you shall die in this instant! Do you bring accusations upon Thomasin Roberts?"

"It is the truth; she conspires to murder the others and escape to the forest with the Devil. She made covenant with him on All Hallows Eve. I saw it with my own eyes."

"Then we shall proceed at once! I will gather the others and we will march to the prison for confirmation."

"For there be no time, she broke the lock and could have already escaped."

Thomas listens to my warning, debating in his head how to proceed. He may not believe me, yet he knows the repercussions of my words holding truth in court. He stares back in the directions of the church and courthouse, and then turns his eyes to the prison. Thomas aggressively pulls me to my feet and begins to choke me. "We shall go to the prison, and if you speak any falsity you will die by my hand immediately!" The squeezing nearly makes me lose consciousness until Thomas relieves his grip.

"I swear it, Reverend, my words will prove as truthful once we enter the cell. She conceals weapons under our mattress and will murder you as soon as you begin inspection."

Thomas no longer pays any mind to my continuous descriptions. While he holds doubt to my every word, he shows enough desperation to return hastily to the prison. I continue to put on quite a performance for Thomas, using the sadness and defeat from the experiences I have gone through on this day. And just as I needed to happen, we continue our journey to the prison without the assistance of any further officials. If Thomas was wise, he would have allowed his men to inspect the cells while I was gone. Yet he must be present, as he takes any moment to torture us and make an example of anyone firsthand.

We have you alone now, Thomas. Proclaiming your plans made this escape much easier to enact. Yet the officials will eagerly await Thomas's return so I must act with haste.

Thomas drags me from the structure, and we begin our journey back to the prison. A striking pain forces me to look down, and I realize that my right hand was submerged in snow and ice after hitting the ground. We sat for a long duration, rendering my hand completely frozen to a sheet of ice under the snow. My adrenaline and desire to trick Thomas prevented me from feeling pain, but Thomas pulling me to my feet ripped layers of skin straight from my hand. Blood pours from below my wrist, bringing on instant dizziness and the desire to faint at any moment. Thomas no longer acts politely or in the same manner as when Mother and Father were present. I fear my shoulder shall break from the force of which I am pulled in these chains. The metal of my chains enters the open wound, and the cold freezes the binding to a stinging frost. This pain becomes unbearable, so I begin to cry natural tears in agony.

"Please, Reverend, I shall follow but you cause me unbearable pain. My hand," I tell Thomas.

Pulling me even harder, Thomas peers back at me in full disgust. "If you are to die then I shall drag thy frozen corpse to the prison. If these accusations hold accuracy, then we must return immediately. And if any witch is to escape the prison, I shall kill you myself for not notifying me prior." Thomas now stops in his tracks to question my words. "Why is it that you held this truth until now?

You could have spoken these words the moment we ventured from the cell, so why turn on thy friends in this instant? Speak of thy deception at once!" Closely studying my every move and reaction, Thomas searches for any sign of panic or lies from my side. I know that my words must come very carefully, or the plan shall fail.

"Because, Reverend, my soul has been saved. My brother is gone, and I have broken free from bewitchment. My mind was influenced by these dark forces, but no longer do I succumb to such wickedness like the others. I understand that Thomasin practices evil behavior, and I wish to take part in it no further. I see it now, and she will kill me for knowing I confessed."

Thomas stares back at me without any emotions. Perhaps my words have instilled fear in the Reverend, as his expression mirrors that on the day he executed Rose. He begins to doubt himself once more and is intrigued, no longer thinking about how he can punish me further. It has been his covert belief from the beginning that there be no witches in The Hollow, but perhaps I have convinced him to question that truth. Thomas turns and continues venturing towards the prison, no longer viciously pulling my arm or rushing.

Thomas may believe that a true witch comes to challenge him, so he must finally face the evil being that he warned our parents of for months.

You knew there be no witches all along, but you used those terms to torture us and brainwash Warren Hollow for your own power and arrogance. Perhaps with a deeper intention we shall never discover. And for the first time, you begin thinking that a witch awaits you and plots to end your life. It has become real to you now, and although I shall never hear you admit those words, I see fear flowing through you, Reverend.

We are but minutes from the prison as the storm rages

around us. My fingers have begun to change color, displaying a blue and gray pattern from the cold. Perhaps I shall lose my fingers and die of sickness after this journey, but the adrenaline rushing through my body prevents the cold from becoming a bother. I feel no more pain and the success of my plans draws near with every step. Thomas has lost himself in his own mind, further distancing his attention from me and my own intentions. Now he only fears the monster that awaits once we reach the cell. But what he doesn't realize is that the only monster he shall face stands right behind him. Convincing Thomas that my cellmate is a witch was quite easy, considering how wise he was to the words of the younger children. While John's intentions were pure, he lacked the knowledge to give the convincing performance that I provided. But I knew to speak the true fears of witchcraft to Reverend Thomas, for us children have discussed and mocked the entirety of all witchcraft accusations from the beginning. Flying through the night, sacrificing children, and using blood to conduct rituals were but jests when spoken amongst us. Yet, these words instill fear, and it is believed by our parents that we hold such capabilities. Thomasin must forgive me for deeming her the most wicked and vile witch of them all, as it will inevitably lead to our freedom.

Please forgive me, Thomasin. While this is a role you shall don well, I only do so to secure our freedom. My only wish is thou not hold this against me.

The day begins to rest as sunlight retreats behind the storm clouds overhead. This blizzard rages on, with no signs of a break in the weather. We draw quite near to the prison, and I fear that I face irreversible damage from spending hours in such conditions. My legs feel as though I drag boulders behind me, each step taking an effort from the lowest of depths. At a glance, my right hand appears to have gone as white as the snow, which is not a positive sign. The expertise of healing that Rose has taught me over the years leads me to believe that I may lose my hand. Similarly, the only feeling in my left hand is the rushing of blood caused from the shackles ripping my skin. I recognize this as positive, knowing that my left hand may survive since we are moments from the prison and complete feeling has not been lost.

John led a positive life every day, regardless of constant illness and impairment. He could barely walk or stand without assistance, yet he remained one of the happiest and joyful individuals across the entire colony. So, I do not mind losing a hand before the nights end, as I only need one to deliver Reverend Thomas his retribution.

The prison now comes into view through the blizzard and the constant voices in my mind go silent. Daytime concludes as the depths of the night will surely surround us in moments. In the rising darkness I find a stillness, recognizing the events that shall unravel as we enter the prison. Months of plotting an escape have led to the arrival of a singular moment. Any signs of fear or panic have vanished from my being, as the time to act is upon us. And for the first time in recent memory, I find myself engaged in a prayer as we reach the entrance to the prison.

Dear God, it has been quite some time. Dost thou remember me? Is it too late to seek thy help? I call out as a doubter and sinner. I beg of thee, guide me through these next few moments and I will be sure to honor your name. I have doubted and seemingly lost all faith, yet I stand here seeking my own redemption. Not that of which Thomas calls for, rather I search for the power to save my friends and rekindle the balance of true faith to our lives. I recognize my defiance, my lord, and cannot deny such resistance any longer. For months I hated thee and felt as though you were the sole reason for our confinement. Yet, I now recognize that you have been present with us from the moment we entered the prison. True faith washes over the cells in the prison, faith in survival and a future, with my friends risking their lives to follow my plans. I ask thee for protection and a chance to shine in thy light. Let me honor John, Ezekiel, and Rose. Lead me through this moment and I shall never doubt my faith again. 'Tis you that has kept me alive and in pursuit of survival. Even without John, I stand full of hope and determination. I could not save him, but this unraveling of events you have provided now gives me the opportunity to save the others. I ask for one final gratuity. Bless me with a miracle, as I fear that is necessary to find success in this improbable solution. Watch over me.

XIII

Divine Intervention

T homas struggles to open the nearly-frozen doors to the prison as I try to regain control of my left hand. One at a time my fingers begin to move and tighten into a fist, blood rushing from the wounds on my arm and wrist. Attempts to revive my right hand fail drastically, as my assumptions were accurate, and I shall lose that hand tonight. None the less I remain focused on the events that are now set in motion.

Here you stand. Your performance has provided the opportunity to have Thomas alone in the prison with all of your friends. Nothing can seemingly go wrong at this point. If only you could have saved John.

My thoughts fight back, but I focus because my life may end in the next few moments. Saving John was a feat of impossibility, yet I can still rescue all my friends if I remain calm. If Thomas discovers my lies, then he will certainly butcher me in front of everyone, or even worse, murder Thomasin as well. The doors to the prison are finally opened and Thomas aggressively pulls me inside by my shackles. Flying through the door, I immediately hit the ground face first with such force to knock the breath from my lungs. My vision becomes blurry, and blood begins to drip into my eyes. Thomas pays me no mind, as he articulately closes each lock and secures the only exit to the prison. He places the keys into his coat pocket, which I shall remember for the near future. Rolling around in a pool of my blood is not a good start to my escape, yet I am still alive and determined to win this battle.

"Rise to your feet or I shall kill you right here," Thomas instructs. I use all the determination in my body to stand, yet I simply cannot. "This be your final warning, Rise at once!" My left hand pushes off the ground, although my right hand has no strength to make any attempt. For the second time my face forcefully meets the ground, angering Thomas enough that he begins to grunt and shout in anger. "So be it, we shall do this by any means necessary," Thomas yells aggressively. He grabs me by my hair and pulls me across the floor of the prison. My chains drag behind as we approach the stairs. Without any hesitation, Thomas throws me down head-first, and I roll the entire way to the bottom.

The awful sights and smells of our confinement meets my violent arrival. It feels as though I have been gone for years, although it was merely a few hours at most. I slowly sit up and stare down the long and dark hallway. My vision is failing but I notice the others peering from their cells.

This cave held you for an unthinkable length of time. Seasons changed and the world continued to evolve while you remained locked away in such darkness. Those nights where you held onto life with everything in your being have led you to this moment. You have grown weak, faithless, fearful, guilty, and defeated while locked away behind these bars. Yet here you are on the other side. Those days of old have passed and you are still alive. You shall never spend another night in this frozen chamber, watching as your friends starve and expire. Finish it.

Thomas makes his way down the stairs, kicking me on his way by and incapacitating me once again. The damage that Thomas has inflicted upon me is unbearable. This moment is undoubtedly the closest I have felt to death, yet I feel the most alive since our gathering in the forest. I have lost so much blood in the past few moments, and I am surprised to see any left as it trickles from my wounds and drips to the ground. Perhaps God is on my side and keeps me alive to fulfill the plans. Perhaps it is my dedication to honoring my brother and freeing the friends I love so dearly. Or perhaps the desire for revenge fuels my every move.

Thomas now pulls me to my feet, holding me in an upright position so we can continue. He quickly wipes the blood from my face and turns my head to whisper in my ear. "Can you hear me?" Thomas says. Slowly I nod my head in acknowledgement. "Very well, then you shall speak the truth when need be." We walk side by side; I stumble through every step as we pass cells with the last of my friends that are still alive. The commotion of my arrival has drawn everyone to the bars in order to watch. We pass Henry and Sam, countless empty cells, a few other children who have shockingly still survived, and we eventually make our way past William and Robert. What was once a prison full of innocent children is now a compact group of survivors. The empty cells remind me of the fate that awaits the rest of them if I am unsuccessful in the coming moments. Too many innocent lives have met their end behind these walls, but now a sinister man shall join them.

Rather than plead and beg as they bear witness to Ezekiel's death, everyone watches in total silence. Disbelief has filled the prison, perhaps from my condition or the composure of Thomas. The whistling of the vicious winds fills the hall, the only sound louder than my own heartbeat.

Focus on the beating of your heart. You are still here; you are still alive.

I feel the Reverend shaking as we now stand face to face with my cell. Thomasin sits on the mattress, nearly frozen in her current state. She raises her gaze and now recognizes Thomas and I. "Emelie?" Thomasin asks with confusion. I nod and begin to cry myself. Thomasin approaches the bars and Reverend Thomas finally reacts. "Keep thy distance, witch!" Thomas shouts angrily. The shouting scares Thomasin and she falls backwards into the wall of the cell. "Now, everyone listen to my words," Thomas begins, "I have been informed of the corruption unfolding in these walls. I know thy plans to escape and corrupt Warren Hollow. And I know it all starts with the witch before me. Thomasin Roberts, reveal thy wickedness. You aim to bewitch the others and murder your Reverend. All Hallows Eve was a devious plan to bring the others into the Devil's grasp. Confess it now or die!"

Thomasin stares back at the Reverend, slowly comprehending the accusations presented to her. Her gaze bounces between mine and Thomas's, almost in a way to beg for interference.

Please forgive me.

"I'm sorry, Thomasin, I told him the truth," I state defeatedly, "Reverend Thomas knows of your deceit. I could not allow you to harm anyone else."

Thomasin breaks into tears at my words. William and Robert begin to speak up in confusion. "Emelie, what is the meaning of this? How could you speak such lies?" William asks. The hall begins to erupt with pleading, some insults thrown at me as well.

Just wait everyone, for my true intentions shall reveal themself.

"Tell him, Thomasin," I exclaim. "He knows of the weapons and thy evil practices."

"Emelie, why would you do this to me? What did Thomas offer thee? Is this for John?"

"John… is dead," I state calmly. My words bring a silence to the prison. Thomasin stares at me in total disbelief, and all pleading for the others has drawn to a calming still.

"It be thy fault, Thomasin, you brought us to the forest and made us engage in such practices. He would be alive if not for your wickedness," I state in accusation.

"Silence thee!" Thomas has heard enough. He throws me backwards and I clash with the bars of William and Robert's cell, falling to the ground once more. "You do not move, or I shall see that you join your brother. And you," Thomas points through the cell bars to Thomasin, "back yourself to the wall at once!"

Reverend Thomas begins to retrieve the keys from his coat pocket. He takes what seems like a few extra moments to prolong entering the cell. Eventually he holds the correct key, his hands shaking near uncontrollably. The key enters the lock and slowly turns to open our cell.

Time to act.

Thomas pulls the cell door wide open, now standing directly with the witch before him. He hesitates for a few moments, unsure of how to approach the situation. They stare at each other motionless, almost waiting for a reaction from the other to proceed. Suddenly, Thomas reaches into another pocket on the inside of his coat. He pulls out a large knife, revealing his immediate intentions. Conducting a trial, or even giving Thomasin a chance to explain herself, has not crossed Reverend Thomas's mind. Rather, he shall murder Thomasin and put an end to what he believes is a powerful witch. William and Robert forcefully attempt to break the lock of their cell to intervene.

"Please, I have done no wrong," Thomasin pleads. Thomas has no thought to give a response, instead he tightens his grip on the blade and starts to approach her. They now stand closer, nearly at arm's reach, and she begins to cower under his presence. "Stay away from me! I am no witch!"

She dives for the mattress to retrieve a weapon of her own, but Thomas reacts and pins her to the floor. Thomasin lies face down with the Reverend kneeling on her from behind. Reverend Thomas realizes he has her under his will and cannot restrain from declaring his victory.

"Alas, not even a witch can combat the power of God. Perhaps it is I that be God in the flesh," he proudly proclaims.

Thomas raises the blade above his head, preparing to deliver a fatal blow. But what the Reverend did not realize is that he has fallen perfectly into my plan. He became so immersed in his own arrogance that he failed to notice me, disobeying his command and now standing directly behind him. I made my way to the window and pulled the largest icicle free during the struggle. Stealthily I approached him from behind and waited for the perfect moment.

And that moment has arrived.

Thomas turns slightly enough to gaze upon me, letting out a gasp in surprise. With all my force I swing the icicle, plunging it directly into his neck before he has a second to react. The sharpness of the ice easily penetrates his skin, nearly exiting the other side of his throat. Immediately he drops the knife and falls to the floor next to Thomasin. He rolls over, struggling at his throat for a few moments as he begins to comprehend what has happened. I meet Thomas's gaze while standing powerfully over him. Within a few moments his struggling begins to slow, and he lays still with eyes wide open, matching my gaze until the end. I watch as he pathetically loses the fight for his life.

I have won.

Thomasin still lies face down, crying uncontrollably while she awaits her death. "Thomasin, 'tis alright. He is not going to hurt you," I say.

I kneel beside her and slowly turn her over to reveal what has occurred. She lets out a scream as she spots the Reverend lying at her side.

"I'm so sorry, I had to get him down here with us. I knew if I could get Thomas alone then I could kill him. Yet the only way was to convince him that you be a witch."

She stares at the Reverend for a few moments, still traumatized and in disbelief of the events that have unfolded over the last few moments.

"Perhaps he wasn't so wise after all, Emelie," Thomasin quietly replies. "Tell me, is it true that John is no longer with us?"

I now lower my guard and allow myself to feel the emotions of the situation. A simple nod is all that I can provide in my current state. Thomasin and I embrace each other for a few moments in silence. She notices my hand and acknowledges the damage I have taken throughout the day.

"How are you still alive?" Thomasin asks, gently placing her hands on my face.

"I needed to save you all. And I made a promise to John. He sacrificed himself with hopes of setting us free. But perhaps it be a miracle. I was chosen to do this and needed to follow through," I reply.

"Well, I'm glad you did, Emelie. You have saved us, let us inform the others."

Thomasin helps me to my feet, and we make our way out of the cell. Those near us witnessed the entire situation, while the others like Samuel and Henry at the end of the hall are still panicking.

"Where is the Reverend?" Henry shouts.

"Emelie killed him," Thomasin states loud enough for everyone to hear. The hall remains quiet for a few moments, then gradually erupts into cheers and shouts of happiness. Recognition of the plan's success calls for immediate relief and celebration. I begin to speak with the last of life in me. "Now…we must act quickly and leave this prison. We –" I pause to spit blood from my mouth and fight my dizziness. "We are to exit The Hollow from the back and make our way to Rose's house in the forest. From there…we shall figure out our next move. Yet the blizzard –" Thomasin holds me up as I start to fall, struggling to wipe the blood from my eyes. "The blizzard rages outside. We must keep each other warm and stay within the darkness of the night in order to make it," I instruct using all of my energy. Then suddenly a strange feeling overcomes my entire body once more. My vision begins to fade, and all the pain quickly follows. I turn to Thomasin, who notices that something is terribly wrong. She begins to panic, but I cannot determine the words that she speaks. Instead, I hear nothing and feel nothing. After a few moments I collapse to the floor, and everything draws into darkness.

I have met my end. Alas, I killed the Reverend and ensured the freedom of my friends. If this is it, then I have fulfilled my wishes. I could not save John, though because of him the others shall see the morning sky as it rises above us. God, I shall never doubt thee again. You have given me the strength to become a hero. Now I can rest.

XIV

Watch Over Me

I feel as though I am lost in a dream, or rather a memory from my past. Perhaps I have reached eternal life in heaven. 'Tis a struggle to open my eyes, as a bright and blinding light hits my face like a swift attack. The sound of rushing water falls upon my ears, alongside the refreshing touch of warmth and comfort. This is the forest, although this forest seems somewhat unfamiliar to me. My memory serves to recognize every leaf and blade of grass within, yet I understand this cannot be the forest of now. Flowers bloom and sun shines down upon me, with animals scavenging all around. Wind gently blows through the trees, cooling my body from the warmth of the sun and moving the branches around me.

Rather than struggling to stand, I effortlessly rise to my feet with ease. My good health has returned, and once more I feel nothing but happiness. Emotions that have since long died in the prison rapidly return, and for the first time in months I cannot fight the urge to smile. I must have escaped to the safest place of my mind, a faultless rendition of nature. A space I have longed for, across every moment of my confinement. This be the place I would venture to upon saving my brother and my friends. But why do I find myself here now? Moments ago, I was breathing my last breaths in the prison, so have I passed into the afterlife?

"Hello?" I curiously say out loud. I begin to walk down the path before me, following alongside the stream as water rushes through the rocks and passages. Gently I use my hands to push a branch out of my way, and I notice that my right hand has also recovered. A few moments pass and I reach a clearing in the brush. Making my way through, I fall into a beautiful opening in the forest that mirrors our location on All Hallows Eve. Immediately I recognize this to be the exact area in which we celebrated that dreadful night, but the darkness concealed its wonderful features back then. My mind starts to recount the horrid memories of that night, visualizing where the assault took place and where I was beaten to the ground. As my emotions begin to shift, a gentle voice calls out and breaks my line of thought.

"You made it!" Shouts of excitement have welcomed my arrival. I aim my eyes in the direction of the voice and let out a gasp of disbelief as I spot my brother, John, sitting near the fire pit. "John," I yell full of emotion, "is that you?"

"Yes, sister, I have waited on your arrival."

Hastily I run as fast as I can to John, embracing him in my arms like never before.

"What a beautiful day," John states happily.

Releasing John from my grasp, I recognize that this moment cannot be real. I look into his eyes, and to my surprise John has risen back to the fullest of health as well.

"John," I say bemused, "where are we?"

John smiles back at me, taking a moment to look around and formulate a response. "We be in the forest, our favorite place."

"Yes, John, but rather what are we? Is this now? Am I dead?"

John stares back with his joy and cheerfulness that has greeted me every day since his birth. "This is the end, sister, yet it is not so bad here," John replies, still holding his enthusiasm.

"I saved them, John. Because of you I freed everyone from Reverend Thomas."

"I saw it. Now we can enjoy this moment together."

John pulls himself closer and rests his head on my shoulder. We sit peacefully, listening to the nature around us and taking in this wonderful moment. For months I spent day and night obsessing over reaching safety with my brother, and we have finally made it. I hold John in my lap, playing with his hair and holding him tight like I have always done when we escaped to the forest. Sometimes we would sit for hours, watching the stream as it went by and taking in all that nature had to offer.

After a short while, John's expression changes and he pulls himself away from my embrace.

"What is it, John?" I ask in confusion.

John smiles back at me and waits briefly before providing a response. "You must go now."

I immediately dispute his words. "No, John, I am not going anywhere. I am to stay here with you. There is so much I need to say." He remains calm and slowly pulls my hand in between both of his.

"For this is good news, sister, 'tis not time for you to be here," he says.

Tears run down my face at John's words. I understand that this shall be the final talk we have together. I do not wish to be anywhere but within this moment here before me.

"And what shall be of you, John?" I ask tearfully.

John once again smiles at my words, excited to provide me with a response. "I will remain here, among the trees in this magical forest of ours. And I shall wait for your return."

And for the second time I must offer a final goodbye to my brother. Although I am overcome by sadness, I understand that this meeting will not carry the sorrow of our prior goodbye. Rather than disputing, I smile back at my brother and match his joy. Taking a few moments to prepare myself, I hold his hand and place value in every moment of this vision.

"Goodbye, John."

My words break the surroundings, and a blinding light overcomes me. I feel an overpowering warmth as though I stand on the sun.

The blinding light suddenly dims to a pit of darkness, and the warmth shifts into a blistering cold upon my skin. Faintly I can hear my name growing louder in my ears. Instantaneously I awaken with a large and forceful gasp for air. Against my wishes, I have returned to the land of the living. My friends stand over me and express relief at my survival.

"Oh, Emelie, I thought thy had left us!" Thomasin rushes to provide comfort and support me as I regain consciousness. Still weakened, I show everyone that I am still here and slowly return to my feet. I realize that all my friends have been released from confinement during my dormancy. Henry, Samuel, William, Robert, Thomasin, and a few other children stand before me, freed from the cells that have housed us for a period of time I cannot determine.

"Emelie," William approaches curiously, "tell us what Thomas hath done to thee. How did you convince the Reverend to come unacquainted?"

I now lean into Thomasin and Henry to keep my balance. With difficulty, I begin to speak in an attempt to ease the tension amongst the group. "I...," beginning in nothing more than a whisper, "I shall explain every detail of the day. But now we must act in haste before our freedom is discovered. We cannot stay in this prison for a moment longer. Gather any weapons and coverings to fend off the blizzard's wrath, and we must leave for Rose's house in the forest at once."

My instructions have taken the last fragment of energy left within me. Henry and Thomasin assist in holding me so that I can lead our escape from the prison. The others begin to gather their weapons, quilts, and anything to prepare for our dangerous escape from these walls. Samuel loots the prison keys from Reverend Thomas's lifeless being, and it seems that our time in the prison has come to an end.

Henry supports my steps as I climb to the first landing of the stairwell. "We must remain together and out of sight. Our safest path is through the back of The Hollow's walls. I have walked a near identical path today, and that shall be our safest option," I explain, spitting out a mouthful of blood.

"And what be of the younger children? Who shall rescue them while we make our escape?" An unfamiliar voice in the group asks. I stand in silence for a moment, recognizing that this would have been the time for John and the others to join us.

"We are the only ones who remain. I shall speak in full once we escape, yet the others have succumbed to the torture," I explain. I watch as the horror of my words hits everybody in the crowd. Some scream and cry out in sadness, as they have just learned that their brothers and sisters passed as well.

Samuel breaks the silence and climbs to join us. "Which key unlocks the prison Emelie?" Samuel asks anxiously. I try to use my right hand and point to the key, now remembering the pure damage of the cold. The frostbite has spread beyond my hand and slowly climbs my arm. Samuel looks at my arm, recognizing the unfortunate situation that must occur.

"Emelie, I'm afraid you must lose that hand if you wish to keep your life. My mother be a wet nurse, and I know that amputation is the only solution," Samuel says.

I stare at my lifeless hand, then slowly direct my gaze to Samuel. "Will I survive?" I ask him curiously with little fear.

"I believe so, Emelie, yet it will be of immense pain and suffering. We shall need an object sharp enough to cut straight through. Perhaps we shall use this," Samuel explains, revealing the blade that Reverend Thomas planned to end Thomasin's life with moments ago.

"Very well, we must journey to Rose's home and get it over with," I reply.

Samuel nods and begins to climb the stairs towards the main entrance of the prison. Thomasin assists Henry once more in supporting my ascent behind Samuel. The others follow close by, marching up the stairs with the same disbelief I shared earlier today. My group of friends has shriveled to near non-existence. Ten children at most have survived the horrors of the prison. In truth I cannot extinguish the burning feelings of guilt as we march away from confinement. Everyone else has lost something in this prison as well, if not their lives. Brothers, sisters, friends, our way of life; but something we all have lost is our parents. Not a single voice from the crowd pleads to visit their old home or make amends with their parents. Perhaps I would have wanted to see Mother and Father, as I could never have imagined the loss of reality inside my home. Every parent made the same choice, following the Reverend and leaving us to rot behind prison walls. My current condition displays full validation of what awaits any child who strays from our plan. Once we arrive at Rose's home, I shall provide a full explanation, killing any doubts or worries among our small group of survivors.

My struggle to climb the stairs has nearly reached its end, so I quickly take one last look down into the horror that has housed us for a period I cannot recollect. Innocent lives were brutally taken inside this captivity. If not from murder, then it be starvation, the weather, weakness, and perhaps lack of hope and loss of faith. I too lost my way in this prison for quite some time. Waiting, perhaps hoping, not to make it to the morning most days. Death would have been a mercy compared to the torture I have faced on this day. I felt anger towards God, refusing to pray or acknowledge his presence. Broken bones, a hand that needs to be removed, losing John, and nearly getting my best friend killed. All things that plague my mind and body right now, yet I cannot fight the feeling of happiness. This torture had a purpose, John's death had a purpose, and my prayers were answered. Of all the other children, I struggle to comprehend why God chose me to guide us all. Rather than question the intentions, I shall cherish the experience I held moments ago as my soul left my body. Perhaps it was but a dream, a hallucination due to injury and blood loss, or perhaps it was a look into the heaven that someday awaits. I can no longer deny that my faith has been restored.

The last of the cells fall out of sight as we finally complete our climb to the top. I respectfully, yet forcefully, push away from Thomasin and Henry. I decline their assistance as they watch me regain my own strength and struggle to stand on my own. Slowly I control my balance, determined to make our escape at my own free will.

"I need to do this," I whisper to Thomasin.

She smiles, understanding that I have earned the struggle of completing my own escape. Samuel studies the door, perhaps anxious of what awaits on the other side. He holds the designated key tightly, directing his gaze to me before proceeding. I look back at the group and then to Samuel, nodding for him to continue.

Without hesitation, Samuel lets out a deep breath and slides the key into the lock. Forcefully he pushes the door, breaking the seal of ice that has since developed due to the storm. Icicles fall and shatter on the outside, and the sounds of the storm grow in intensity as wind prevents the door from opening without struggle. With one final push, the door opens, and we are met by a swarm of snowfall. 'Tis a beautiful sight, because our time in the prison has come to an end.

XV

At The Helm

The blizzard has gradually worsened since my return, making this journey nearly impossible. Although dangerous, we must prevail and quickly exit the prison before the Reverend's disappearance raises suspicion. Thomas planned on returning to the church earlier in the day, even trying to stop there before sending me back to the prison. Hopefully the storm continues to conceal his true whereabouts, and the chaos remains unknown long enough for us to escape. Perhaps they assume he nervously waits for the storm to end in his home or unharmed elsewhere.

They are going to come looking for the Reverend and catch us all in the snow. If we are spotted, then everything will be revealed. Do not think of this current situation as freedom. But when will true freedom be achieved?

The voice in my head returns once more to doubt our plan and cause me agony. Yet I listen to this voice, as it provides reason and realism to the situation we face. We must act with haste to survive. If the officials do not murder us, then the storm certainly will. Most of us hang on tightly to life as it could very well end at any moment. Somehow, we carry on, comforting each other and preparing to embark on our journey through the storm. William has created a makeshift link of chains for us to stay together and find our way. We slowly move into position, Samuel understanding my determination and taking his place in line behind Thomasin.

"Emelie, are you certain you want to lead us into the forest?"

Thomasin shouts over the wind.

I look back and answer her with conviction. "Yes, Thomasin, for I have walked this path since my days of infancy. I have snuck through the shadows and could walk the path if my eyes be closed. And I have made this journey earlier today, perhaps I can follow Thomas and I's footsteps. We must pass our homes and exit through the back gate," I say.

"Very well," Thomasin answers submissively, "lead us to our freedom. I shall be right behind thee."

I take one final look at our group and suddenly feel anxious. More so than when the Reverend took me, or even when I ended his life. Now I am solely responsible for the life of every person behind me, and I must lead them to freedom.

The hard part is over, you shall arrive at Rose's home, and they will be forever grateful to your efforts. But do not forget the situation that awaits your arrival.

I look down at my hand, remembering the mutilation I shall withstand once we escape The Hollow. The others wrapped my hand in cloth, preventing further damage and concealing the horror from my sight. Rather than holding the chains in my hands again, I tightly wrap the link around my waist so that I can lead without looking back. The others secure the chain in their hands and the time to move has come. We start to take steps away from the prison, leaving the last of the shelter until we arrive at our destination. The only guide before me is the illumination of the snow in the darkness. Few lanterns light the surrounding structures, but the wind forces our gaze to the ground.

Everyone works together to proceed through the storm, providing comfort and reassurance to those around them. We have survived too long and fought for this freedom; the cold cannot take us now.

Look at how far you have come. Perhaps the most natural witch in Warren Hollow, hiding in the woods and living in a fantasy of nature. Some used to make jest of your ways, now you guide their very survival. Backed fully with their trust and the hope to find a normal life once more. You hold a responsibility of which was not desired, and you murdered a man on this day. But 'tis you chosen to lead. Perhaps by God, or perhaps by your own desires and a longing for justice.

Each step requires an abundance of energy that most of us lack. The chain pulls me and slows my movement to agonizing individual steps. Taking a quick glance back, I cannot see faces past Thomasin and Samuel. The winds are too vicious, and the snow eliminates nearly all visibility. Under my breath I continue to repeat the same words to myself.

"Keep going...keep going...keep going."

We must push forward, through the exhaustion, weather, and fear. I simply cannot rest until we escape the walls of The Hollow, but even so what be the plan once we reach Rose's homestead? Do we run forever, and how long will this witch hunt last? Surely the others will want us dead after discovering the Reverend. But these are worries for a later day, not presently as we march through a fatal storm.

"Look everyone," Thomasin yells, "we are passing through the center of the village."

Directing my gaze at her instruction, we stand just before the platform of execution. I stare emotionless as the brutality we faced months ago begins to fill my mind. Everyone was captive in chains, forced to wear masks and helplessly watch our dear friend's murder. A single rope swings from the tree, tied in a noose and looking to take another life at any given moment.

Live by your own desires.

Rose's words pierce through my brain just as they did on that horrible day. It's as though she is here with us, making her presence known and leading us to freedom.

"We must keep moving, we are going in the right direction thus far," I shout back.

"Very well. Everyone, stay close and we must keep going!" Samuel yells to the rest of the group to inform them of my words.

Our journey continues, but something feels strange. My steps begin to feel lighter, and the force of the wind has seemingly disappeared. Nervously I raise my eyes, and the sting of snowfall does not force my face to the ground.

"No," I say under my breath. To my horror, the storm looks as though it is passing.

This cannot be, our cover will vanish and surely we will be seen within minutes. As the storm slows, our parents and the officials will set out to find Thomas, discovering that we have escaped our confinement.

"Thomasin, the storm is coming to a halt! We are to be seen and our lives will be taken," I exclaim in a panic.

"Emelie, what are we to do? We must act quickly!"

The group begins to panic, plotting to run frantically or to hide in nearby structures. For the first time I fail to devise a strategy. My plans have worked perfectly up until this moment, but surely we will be caught if I do not formulate a fast solution.

The voice in my head has gone silent, and I desperately look to the others for guidance.

Henry climbs onto the platform in an attempt to restore order to the group. "We cannot panic! For the storm shall only conceal our position for a few more moments. The sun soon rises, so we must either hide or run for our lives."

"I have an idea," Samuel quietly expresses from the crowd, "we can hide under the courthouse in the cells. When they took us months ago for interrogation, the basement was fit to be a prison. That shall provide shelter and hide us as we wait for the storm to continue."

"That may be unwise, Samuel," Robert says in protest.

Thomasin raises her hand to draw attention. "I agree with Samuel. We simply cannot run through The Hollow without the storm. They will see us and then we will die. If we hide, even for an hour, then perhaps the storm will strengthen, and we can make our escape."

I ponder the options for a few moments, not wanting responsibility for the outcome of any choices. For a few moments I listen in silence as the group debates and covers various plans. Samuel directs his gaze to me, coming close enough to whisper in my ear.

"Trust me, Emelie," Samuel pleads.

Samuel has faith that the courthouse shall be our best option, so I nod in agreement. He smiles, respecting my confidence in his plan as he climbs the steps of the platform.

"And Emelie, what say you?" Samuel raises his voice loud enough to gather everyone's attention.

Silence falls over the crowd as every face now stares at me desperately. Rather than directing the group, Samuel allows me to have the final say. I look around at everyone and begin to agree with Samuel. "We must not stay here. Follow Samuel to the courthouse, we shall hide and wait for the storm to continue. That be our safest option. We will escape by sunrise and leave this village behind," I say.

I unwrap the chains from my waste and prepare to run. "Samuel, lead us to the courthouse."

Samuel smiles as the attention draws back to him. "Everyone, stay close and keep up. We are not far from the courthouse, so we must move swiftly!" Everyone begins to remove all bindings. Moments prior we held onto the makeshift chain as if it was our lifeline, but as the storm clears we can see straight through the night. One by one the others stretch and prepare for the sprint that awaits. Our energy is low, and fear runs high, so we must act without hesitancy. I ponder on my struggle to climb the stairs no more than an hour ago, further fearing our sprint. Blood still pours from my wounds, and pain radiates throughout my entire body. 'Tis difficult to breathe properly as well, and certainly I suffer from broken bones and other injuries. But a true leader would guide this escape and act with bravery until the end.

You can do this. There is no need for doubt.

Reassurance within reminds me that my friends depend on me, placing all faith in their survival through my choices. "We must act in haste, but also in complete silence. Follow Emelie, be sure to stay within the shadows and away from light. I shall use the Reverend's keys to gain access to the courthouse," Samuel tells the group.

I come forward in agreement. "Aye, perhaps we shall wait there for a few minutes, or perhaps we shall wait until sunrise. Once the storm gathers in strength then we will make our way to the back exit of the village."

Looking at Samuel, I signal that it is time to leave this exposed area. Thomasin comes beside me, providing comfort and just enough support while also allowing me to stand on my own.

Henry watches as well, giving me the space I desire but also staying within reach if I am to collapse. And without hesitation, we start to run.

Samuel leads just before me, Thomasin and Henry close behind. Robert places himself at the back of our group, prepared to defend if we are to be chased. To my surprise, I can run at a brisk pace with little issue. My legs match my breath and I have gained enough momentum to achieve full speed. We traverse through the snow, sliding across ice and nearly falling from every step. The wind stings my face, burning my skin and forcing my gaze to the ground once more. Yet, I feel a rush of joy as we make our way through the narrow path to the courthouse. I have not wandered through the outdoors in months, and my memory falls back to the times of endlessly running and galloping through the forest. John used to love high speeds while adventuring beyond The Hollow. We would run through the trees and brush on the riverside until my legs could carry us no further. Oh how I long for those simple, wonderful days.

Gradually the courthouse comes more and more into view. Some of the others slow down and struggle as we reach our final pass of running. I also feel the desire of falling to the ground, yet the risk of being spotted deters my rest as we are but moments away.

Thoughts fill my mind, preventing me from noticing our frightening surroundings. Most of Warren Hollow is lost to complete darkness. No fires or lanterns to light the homes that held immeasurable joy in the past. My late-night returns to the village would be greeted with fires, some laughter and banter from those awake and drinking until the morning, and beautiful lanterns illuminating the dark. The Hollow always rested upon nightfall, but never to the extent of what I witness now.

This place is no longer home, my home is what I shall make it with those just behind me.

"We've made it," Thomasin shouts in joy.

Cautiously we gather near the back entrance of the courthouse, Samuel eagerly searching for the proper key. I scan the area in a panic, watching for anyone to have followed us or spot us from their homes. To my surprise there is not a single sound.

"Got it," Sam tells the group.

He twists the key and forces the door open. Directly on the other side is a stairwell leading to the basement, nearly identical to the stairs of the prison.

"We shall not stay here long," I say to the group, perhaps trying to convince myself that this next prison is only temporary. "Lead the way, Samuel."

Samuel begins to descend the stairs, but suddenly halts in a way that signals his true fear. Memories of the horror he faced in this courthouse flush back into his mind, replaying as if it is occurring once more presently. Months ago, he saw plenty of our friends murdered in this very structure. This is a terror I recognize, as I felt an identical force upon reentering the prison. 'Tis hard not to blame thyself or pray for a different outcome, yet the past cannot be changed. I place my hand on his shoulder to provide reassurance and calm his nerves.

We reach the bottom, entering a broad opening with cells across the perimeter. This is undoubtedly an improvement from our conditions in the actual prison. The middle of the room is large enough for everyone to gather and remain close. A few of the others devise a plan to keep watch on the doors and windows, waiting for anyone to approach or for the storm to worsen.

I begin searching through the numerous boxes and supplies

that are scattered throughout the basement. Thomasin shouts in joy upon discovering a large pile of rations. Clothing, jars of food and old vegetables, and even some medicines are lined neatly in a few crates. Rather than rushing to claim what has been found, everyone waits and draws their attention to me, looking for approval or allowing me to go first. They are foolish to think I am any more deserving than any of them.

"We must take what we can. But first we must eat until we cannot handle another bite," I reassure the group in order to provide relief. The food may be spoiled and out of season from the summer farming months, but we smile and eat as though we have never eaten before.

"Can you believe it, Emelie? God be with us on our journey," Thomasin claims.

"Aye, perhaps it is a miracle. One we so desperately needed," I reply.

One by one we gather plentiful portions of food, as any supplies in our journey ahead are quite uncertain. Robert and William take their portions and begin keeping watch at the door. The others prepare for much needed rest, but I notice that Samuel is not with the group. I start to search for him, walking away from the group and into the back corners of the basement. Momentarily I lay eyes on Samuel, who stares emotionless into an empty cell. Respectfully I approach him from behind, he notices me and attempts to break away from his thoughts.

"This is where they held us, Emelie. Ezekiel and all the others. When they came for us, I hid around this corner like a coward. I could hear everyone above us, all the officials and our parents. I waited for hours, watching the torment and eventual slaughter. Reverend Thomas explained to the crowd how the trial would unfold, yet most parents shouted for our execution with no further explanation necessary. I heard my own parents as well, Emelie," Samuel explains.

"I am sorry, Samuel. You are not a coward, you knew what awaited upstairs," I reply.

"I tried to talk all of them out of it while we waited. They would not listen as I pleaded for them to act calmly. Instead, they wanted to fight and so I simply hid, yet there was honor in supporting my friends instead of hiding like a frightened child."

I stare at Samuel, searching for any way to provide comfort and help to heal his pain. "This be a pain I understand, Samuel," I express calmly, "I have yet to inform the others, but the Reverend took me to my home today. He used my brother's final moments of living to torture me more than any physical pain ever could."

Samuel stares in disbelief. "And how did John find his way back to your home?" He asks.

"He was the last remaining child after the officials forced death upon them. They were starved and deprived of adequate living conditions. John knew he was going to die, so he used his final moments to make confession to free us all."

Reliving the torture of my brothers passing causes immense sadness. "My parents welcomed his confession, placing more focus on his false truth than his health. Mother smiled upon his passing, and that's when I knew that we needed to escape and never return to our parents. The people we remember are now a memory, manipulated through fear and corruption from Reverend Thomas. But here we stand, moments from an escape made possible through the sacrifices of John and Ezekiel and Rose. The Reverend lays dead in the prison and we shall never spend another night in chains. I must tell the others these very words, that is if losing my hand does not take my life as well," I say.

Samuel pulls me closer, reassuring that I shall live and make a recovery. The panic of escaping has prevented any further thought into nearly losing my life on the prison floor. Perhaps staying in that place with John was death itself, and I felt ready to accept such a conclusion. But now is not the time to ponder, we must get out of these village walls for the others to be safe.

"Quiet!" Henry interrupts our conversation with a panicked command. "Someone approaches the door. Be gone with all light and hide yourselves!"

Everyone rushes to stoke the lanterns that provide our only light and warmth. Henry and William stand by the door, waiting for everyone to hide out of sight. We panic, unsure of who approaches or how many of them.

Did they see us? Has Reverend Thomas's body been found? How will we escape from this basement?

XVI

A Light In The Dark

Rather than continuing my panic, I calmly ask Henry for information in order to ease the tension. "What can you see, Henry? How many approach us?"

Henry peers through the door's small window cautiously to remain hidden. "It looks as though there be two of them. They come slowly, 'tis hard to recognize them given the snow."

"Yes," William says while pushing Henry aside, "the storm now rages like when we left the prison. We must get out of here quickly. But these men draw near, everyone hide!"

We retreat around the corner on the far side of the basement. It would be foolish to believe we are in any condition to stand our ground and fight. Most of us suffer from injury and exhaustion, given our previous sprint and all that we have endured. Reverend Thomas has inflicted enough damage on my body that the next injury may very well be my last. Yet I peer around the corner, watching as Henry and William await on the inside of the door. They stand on either side of the small passage that connects the door to the stairway. Samuel and Robert stand just behind me, armed with knives to defend the few of us unable to fight if need be.

A slight turn of the doorknob breaks the silence like the gunfire on All Hallows Eve. We all hold our breath as the door begins to open. The shine of a lantern breaks through the darkness and immediately I freeze.

"Reverend, are you down there?" a mysterious voice asks.

"He's not down there, idiot, doth thou see any light or signs of him?" another responds.

"The door was open, so he must have stopped here on his way back. We both saw the footprints, so we should check if he be down there."

The voices are those of two officials. It appears that concern grows for the Reverend's whereabouts. Members of The Hollow must be searching for Thomas since the storm began to subside. Still I hold my breath, listening as the two men make their way down into our basement.

"Look, I told you he must be here," one of the men says. "This lantern is hot to the touch, and these rations are out of order."

The men begin to search through the main area that we all sat in moments ago. There was no time to hide the lanterns or rations of food, so our presence is obvious, and suspicion remains at a high.

"Let's search through this courthouse then. If Reverend Thomas stopped here, then he may have found trouble. You go search the grounds while I go through these hallways. Come back once you search every room of the court," The man instructs.

After a few moments of debate, one of the men makes their way back up the stairs. The door abruptly opens and slams as he leaves the basement.

"There's just one of them now, Emelie," Samuel whispers, "I shall wait for the right moment to engage with him."

Samuel stands ready to attack as the man grows near. Light from the lantern dances across the walls as the man maneuvers through the basement. He begins to search the cells and corners of the basement, closely analyzing all the shadows and hiding places. Yet he does not search for us, he is looking for a single man in the Reverend. To our surprise, the light stops moving and the man appears to take a seat. Carefully I peak my head around the corner, and the man has in fact decided to rest. Rather than continuing the search, he begins to scavenge through the rations just like us. He finds a bottle of alcohol and drinks it intensely. Suddenly he turns his head, nearly spotting me as I pull back around the corner.

"He saw me, Samuel," I say, "he knows we are here."

Samuel pushes me behind him, taking a brave stance just at the corner of the wall. He draws the knife above his head, preparing to redeem his cowardice and attack the second the man comes our way.

"Reverend, is that you?" The man asks. He gets back to his feet and drops the empty ale to the floor. Raising the lantern for light, the man slowly makes his way to our position. "Are you hurt, Thomas?"

The man walks closer, his lantern illuminating the growing shadow on the wall before us. Footsteps become louder, and Samuel tenses up in preparation of his attack.

"It would be wise not to move any further!" Henry yells.

I hear a gasp, and suddenly the movement stops in our direction. Silence falls across the basement, so I glance back around the corner. The man stands just on the other side of the wall, Henry and William holding a knife to his throat. Fear fills the man's face; he holds his hands in the air to signal a surrender.

"Please," the man begs, "I do not wish to harm you."

William directs the man to move as Henry holds the knife steady in position. Slowly they walk him back to the chair, instructing him to take a seat. Nervously the man agrees, doing exactly as told.

"What is going on here?" The man asks, confused and frightened. His face lights up in surprise as the rest of us reveal ourselves from behind the wall. The man stares at each of us, wondering how he found himself in such a position.

"How… did all of you come to be down here, in such weather? Wait…" suddenly he realizes who we are. "It is you, all of you. Or at least what be left of the children. Please lower the knife son, I mean no harm," he pleads.

Henry looks at each of us, and I cannot help but trust the man's words. He is afraid, appearing harmless. I nod at Henry, and cautiously he lowers the knife but keeps it steady in his hand. Henry and William stand over the man as he sits in the chair. He goes to speak, then suddenly stops himself to grab the bottle of ale. The man raises the bottle above his head to take a drink, forgetting that the bottle is empty. Anxiously he laughs, dropping the bottle to his side. "The Reverend," he asks, "hath any of you seen Thomas?"

We look at each other, nobody wanting to speak and break the silence. After a few more seconds I decide to move forward.

"Aye, he is over in the prison," I say. The man stares back at me, attempting to make sense of my words.

"In the prison," He repeats in confusion, "then how are all of thee here?"

"Reverend Thomas came to bring us his usual torture and manipulation. I waited patiently for the right moment, then I plunged an icicle through his neck." Slowly I move closer to the man. "Once he was dead, we took his keys and made our escape."

To my surprise the man shows no increased signs of fear, but rather curiosity. He looks around the room at everyone, then slowly raises his gaze to me.

"You…you killed Thomas?" He asks. I nod, providing validation to the worst just spoken. "And how did you find yourselves in this courthouse?"

I continue to provide the fullest truth to our prisoner. "We were using the wickedness of the storm to conceal our escape. Then as the storm began to slow, we needed a shelter until the conditions worsened once more."

The man sits in silence, taking in all the information I have just provided. He starts to speak, but decides to pause his words and reach through the rations. Henry and William stay ready to restrain the man, yet he simply reaches for another bottle of ale.

"The storm has worsened out there, so you best be on your way," The man says. His words strike all of us with surprise, as our confession of murder and escape has drawn little reaction. "Thomas is dead by his own doing," he mutters to himself, "I cannot determine a fate more deserving for such a false prophet."

We all look at each other, shocked by the man's response to our crimes. "I told them all he was of ill mind," the man says to himself, "most followed his words but there were a few who did not take to his teachings. It all happened in such haste."

I stare at the man, attempting to understand his words. "So you did not care for the Reverend?" I ask.

He shakes his head in disapproval. Suddenly anger begins to fill my body, but I prevent myself from lashing out.

"In the days and months that we sat in prison, while the younger children starved and died, there were others who felt it was unjust? Why did they stay quiet, letting the Reverend manipulate everyone and slaughter us one by one?" I ask.

"I am new to Warren Hollow, but from my understanding the witchcraft accusations did not stop when you all faced imprisonment. At first everyone followed Thomas's words, listening to the message and believing that confessions shall be the answer." The man leans forward in the chair. "But that be only the beginning of the horror in your village. They stuck together, parents holding to faith and praying for the redemption of their children. Then Thomas gathered everyone in Warren Hollow for the beginnings of your trial in this very courthouse," The man says.

That was the night when many of our friends died. Our parents held onto their faith until that night, hoping that we could seek salvation and rid the Devil from our souls. The events that unfolded in this structure proved our guilt in their eyes, but this provides no explanation for his hatred towards the Reverend.

I continue to question the man. "And how did that night cause a fallout among our parents?"

He hesitates, nearly afraid to proceed with his words. Though sensing our impatience, he continues to cooperate and answer my questions. "Not long after that night," the man speaks nervously, "your parents began to accuse each other of bewitchment. One by one, accusations began to fly around Warren Hollow."

I find little shock in his words. It should be no surprise that our parents would eventually accuse each other as they have done to us.

The man continues. "The apothecary was dead, and all the children were to seek redemption in prison, yet everything worsened and the wickedness grew in strength. If illness prevented a family from attending church, they must be tangled in bewitchment and conjuring specters at home. If crops failed to produce, then the farmhand practiced evil to intentionally damn the farm for personal thrill. I have seen such terrors repeating through the years." The man fights back tears with all of his strength. "Husbands and wives accused each other, just as they have done to their children. Families torn apart, when there be not a witch as far as the land goes," The man admits.

We now have validation and support of our innocence for the first time in months. Although words of support have remained silent among the last few sensible occupants of The Hollow. Our brothers and sisters faced death, parents lost to blind faith, and now we run for our lives towards a world of unknowns.

Looking closer at the man I begin to recognize that he appears much different than the other church officials. My curiosity overcomes me, so I simply ask the man one final question.

"Who are you?"

The man surveys the crowd around him, again showing signs of fear as though his identity shall seal his fate. Regardless he slowly rises to his feet, prompting everyone to raise their defenses once more. Hesitantly he begins to undo his large coat to reveal a uniform underneath. We all gasp upon discovering that the man wears a white band around his neck, and a cassock that reaches the ground. Standing in total disbelief, we now realize that this man is much more than a regular official.

"My name is Gregory Ordeux...Reverend Gregory Ordeux if you will."

"You are a Reverend?" I ask.

"Perhaps on most days, child. But on this cold evening I am but a drunken friend, that I promise," The man replies.

Another Reverend? He cannot possibly seek to save us while Thomas wished to torture us to death.

"What brings you to The Hollow, Gregory?" Samuel asks sternly. "Was not one Reverend enough to butcher us all?"

Gregory sits back down to lower the tension before he answers Samuel.

"I have been appointed by higher forces to travel to Warren Hollow with the hopes of restoring order," Gregory says, "rumors have spread far and wide of a farming village destroyed from the inside by witchcraft, perhaps the most affected plantation in all the colony. And all I have found upon my arrival is death at the hands of a Reverend gone mad. Proper procedure has not been followed by your Reverend. I have been here but a weeks' time and have yet to lay eyes on a true witch, even down here today. So please, would someone be so kind as to tell me how such foolishness truly began?"

"All Hallows Eve," I say before anyone else takes the opportunity. "Fear was spreading day after day through The Hollow because Thomas imprisoned our apothecary on counts of practicing witchcraft, and by All Hallows Eve we were on a lockdown. Our parents already held onto Reverend Thomas's words out of fear and faith, then they caught us sneaking out and celebrating in the forest. We know it be a mistake, but we would not have left The Hollow if we knew what punishments awaited us," I recall emotionally.

William begins to question Gregory's identity. "And why would they send another Reverend to restore order? Obviously Reverend Thomas paid no mind to your authority."

"Aye, he did not take well to my arrival. Yet I held no choice in the matter of coming to this village, as I hold knowledge on witchcraft higher than many in this world. I have spent years in Europe, aiding in trials and proceedings across many witch hunts. Within New England more recently. The courts are in shambles and 'tis proper faith that shall restore rationality. And while your tale involves sin and murder, I find that nobody in this village is bewitched," Gregory says.

I sense our conversation slowly drawing to a close, and feelings of fear and anxiousness fill my body once more. He knows we murdered Thomas, so he will certainly send us back to prison.

"So, what is to become of us? We shall not return to that prison for another moment of time. Let us go and we will never return to these walls," I state.

Gregory notices my fear and raises his hands to ease the tension once more. "I sense I hold no power in this matter." Gregory looks at each of our faces to verify his thoughts. "Thou would not go back to the prison by free will. It is not my intention to imprison you all. False imprisonment is not justice in the eyes of God. Yet a crime was committed, and a Reverend was murdered. And if village rules were followed then we may not stand here today." Gregory pauses to stand. "But Thomas brought about his own fate through his own devilish behavior. Children being children should not condemn them to a rope around their throats. Will you all do as I say in this desperate moment?" He asks.

We all look at each other, unsure of what Gregory requests of us. He knows that we will not follow him willingly to the prison, for he would sentence himself to death if he forcefully tried to make us return. But he appears reasonable and determined to undo the damage in Warren Hollow.

"Ask what you will," Samuel says.

"A simple request," Gregory replies, "something that keeps us all alive on this night. As I said just minutes ago, you all should be on your way." Gregory looks out of the small window near the door. "The storm has worsened, allowing you to continue your escape as planned. The sun shall rise within the hour. You cannot stay in this village, for they shall hang you all once Thomas's body is found. If you would let me go, I shall not speak of this meeting. Would thou give me the chance to save thy home and undo the harm of Thomas?"

How can we trust Gregory's words? Perhaps he has tried to save himself through false promises and kindness. But we cannot harm an innocent man. If he is honest and true to his word, killing him would make us but as evil as Thomas.

"Very well," I say, "there be no witches amongst us. Only survivors fighting to find the life we desire. Perhaps you can save this village and recover whatever is left of our parents. We shall make our exit at your departure."

We begin to gather any rations and make our way for the stairs. Even Gregory slips another bottle of ale into the pockets of his covering. The others keep their gaze locked on him, not fully trusting his honesty. I notice that Samuel has not moved towards the stairs. He stands once more, staring into the empty cell that has haunted him day and night. "Samuel, we are to move quickly," I tell him.

"I simply cannot, Emelie," Samuel replies. His words draw the attention of the others and silence falls across the basement. "I must take control of my fate, so I choose to stay here."

"They will kill you, come with us and we can be free from this place," I plead.

"Allow me to make this sacrifice, Emelie. I shall take the blame for Reverend Thomas's demise and plotting the escape. This will give me the chance to stand before our parents and tell the truth of the matter."

"They will not want to hear it," Thomasin yells, "our parents are too far gone. Come with us, please!"

Gregory positions himself between Samuel and the rest of the group. He turns to Samuel, placing his hand on his shoulder. "Son, I cannot guarantee your safety for confessing to such a crime. Yet if you choose to stay, I shall do everything in my power, and the power of God, to influence a fair trial and recover Warren Hollow from hell."

Gregory turns his attention to the rest of us, waiting for someone to respond. Thomasin begins to cry, fearful that our dear friend Samuel shall die like the many others who have taken such a stand.

I walk past Gregory and embrace Samuel in my arms. This sacrifice he aims to make is one I truly understand. From the moment we found ourselves locked in the prison I understood my purpose. Now Samuel finds himself determined to confront the horrors faced in this courthouse and take the action he refused to in the past. The others simply do not understand this need to fulfill such a craving for justice, yet I know it quite well.

"I understand," I whisper to Samuel. "Do what you must, and we shall meet once more."

Samuel pulls away, nodding approval to my words. He reaches into his coat and reveals the Reverend's knife, preparing to advise what must be done with my hand. Rather than allowing him to speak, I simply retrieve the blade from his hands, indicating that I do not need a final explanation. Thomasin and the others rush to Samuel while I draw my attention to Gregory.

"Thank you, Reverend…thank you for seeing us for what we are," I say.

Gregory nods, giving equal gratitude for the sparing of his life. Perhaps he shall restore order to our village and put an end to this outlandish witch hunt. The state of the other colonies across New England remains unknown to us, and we have lost all recollection of the time that has passed while we sat in prison. Other communities may return to normal life, or they could descend into madness alongside ours. Most parents and adults of The Hollow deeply believed in Thomas and his progress, so Gregory must defy the odds and somehow restore normalcy and undo months of destruction. His task proves nearly impossible, so we shall not remain and wait for a victory.

This stop in the courthouse has resulted in us losing Samuel, a vital member of our group and a true leader. Yet I feel as though we were drawn to this location to meet Gregory. Perhaps a higher power guides us, as meeting this new Reverend could play a vital role in our survival. If Samuel has enough faith to sacrifice himself, then I shall remain optimistic as well. Regardless, our goal has remained unchanged, and the escape in motion must proceed. We quickly begin to gather any final rations and redress with our coats and coverings. Gregory explains the details to Samuel of how to proceed once they leave the courthouse. Samuel will fully submit to Gregory, and they shall create a believable tale of how he came to be in the courthouse. Personally, I feel that the truth holds enough power in itself to justify our actions and open the eyes of our parents.

Gregory fastens a restraint around Samuel's hands, acting as though he truly discovered an escaped prisoner. They make their way to the stairs, both taking one final look before venturing into the cold. Gregory turns his attention towards me and offers one final remark to our group.

"May God be with you," he says compassionately.

Henry and William use their strength to force open the basement door as a gust of wind fills the air. The storm has regained its full power, so we must leave in the coming moments. Samuel smiles as the door closes, and I pray this will not be the last time we lay eyes on him.

Have faith in the good of Gregory and Samuel. Perhaps the words of Samuel will not hold any power, yet the words of a Reverend may undo the work of another.

We hear the commotion of Gregory and Samuel reentering the courthouse. "Get over here and help me," Gregory says. The footsteps of the other man rush above our heads. "Who is this? I assumed the basement to be empty!" The other man exclaims.

A loud bang indicates Samuel being thrown to the ground. "I found him hiding in the far corner. And there be a major issue! This boy says he attacked Thomas and fled from the prison. Gather everyone you can and go there at once, I suspect the others have fled as well. I shall stay here and uncover more of the truth while I await your return!"

The other man remains speechless, and after a few moments his rushed footsteps move towards the main entrance of the courthouse. Forcefully the door slams behind him, and now it is time to make our escape.

With the intensity of the storm we must regroup in similar fashion, one child in front of the other. We are quite close to the back gate of the village, yet with the sun rising there be no other choice than to move as quickly as possible. Cautiously I gaze from the door, making sure that there are no other officials or parents to cross our path. The storm nearly eliminates all visibility, which is exactly what we needed to conceal our escape.

"The time has come," I tell the others, "for the sunrise is

near so we must move quickly."

Forcefully I pull the door wide open, and without hesitation we leave the basement and find ourselves in the storm once more. Adrenaline fills my body as freedom finally grows closer. We begin to run, faster than before and on pure survival instinct. Reaching the village walls will ensure our freedom and we do not intend to die after making such progress. Minutes pass although they feel like hours, but we never slow down. All pain and fatigue are ignored as the edge of The Hollow comes into visible distance.

"We are nearly there, 'tis just past these houses so we must keep going!" I yell.

Suddenly the events of the previous day begin to crowd my mind as we approach our homes. This is the path that led to my brother's death, but today we will travel farther. I will pass without taking so much as a glance at my home, as I have burned this place to the ground in my mind. The pain of entering the delusions of my parents and watching my brother die is something that shall haunt me for the rest of my days. One by one we pass by our homes, and within a few moments mine comes into view. Staying true to my beliefs, I divert my gaze to the path before me. Although ignoring the presence of the beautiful place that once was draws emotion from within.

I think of the perfect family that once lived happily within those walls. Parents who loved their children and did whatever necessary to nurture and care for a sick child. The years I spent playing with John and helping father chop wood or helping mother prepare meals. Endless nights in my room spent fantasizing about nature, and eventually the countless escapes from every accessible door and window. This is where I grew up, maturing to the person I am today from birth. I find peace in understanding that one single night would not have caused the torture I have endured. Refusing to join the festivities on All Hallows Eve would not have kept me from prison or saved my brother. We may have saved ourselves a few days out of confinement, but our relationship with Rose and the madness of Reverend Thomas would have eventually caught up to us. There was never an escape from the catastrophe that unfolded in Warren Hollow.

As we pass my home, I use all my power not to give in and take one final look. My emotions have mixed between the good and bad experiences, but I understand that everyone behind me is suffering as well. The others have lost parents, brothers, sisters, and their entire lives due to accusations of witchcraft. Watching Samuel and the words of Gregory has given me faith, allowing me to move forward with hopes of a better future.

"God, please care for Samuel and save our village," I whisper under my breath.

In truth, I hold fear for the path ahead. Part of me wishes to turn around and join Samuel back in the prison, because the future remains unclear as we venture into the unknown.

What shall we do if Samuel is murdered, and they come looking for us? Reverend Gregory may not hold enough power to restore The Hollow to the days of old. Or even worse, what are we to do if Gregory is successful and the witch hunt comes to an end?

I have dived so deeply in my thoughts, failing to realize that we have reached our destination. The exit of the village lies just before us. Perhaps all the officials have rushed to the prison, or maybe they no longer guard any entrances and exits of The Hollow. Rather than scaling the wall or using the caution I do on our nighttime escapes, I simply push the gate open so we can walk straight through. Effortlessly we all move to the outside and slam the gate behind us.

Some of the others fall to the ground out of pure exhaustion. Pain creeps back into my body and I find myself collapsing to the ground as well. We ran as fast as possible, ignoring the weather and giving full effort to survival. This moment's rest has been earned, and after months of plotting we have officially reached the outside.

XVII

By The Grace of God

Nobody dares to speak a word and disrupt the intensity of such a beautiful silence. We sit fatigued, staring at each other and gasping for air. In this state of exhaustion, I believe that stopping at the courthouse ensured our survival. Reverend Gregory or any others out on a search would have spotted us, as we may have collapsed inside the village walls. Gregory listened closely to our words and promised us a better future, yet those promises could have transpired to ensure his own safety. He knew that stating anything in contradiction could have cost him his life. But I believe Gregory to be honest, and every word spoken in the basement was pure. Thomas was frozen with fear while confronting a so-called witch in the prison. If Gregory believed in such foolishness, then he may have dropped dead at a first glance of our group.

I rise to my feet, prepared to move forward and never return to the place of my birth. The others notice my actions and slowly follow.

"Maybe Gregory shall restore order to this place," Thomasin says. "Samuel held faith so I will as well."

Although I have spent months plotting to escape this place and never return, it is hard to deny my emotions. A higher power guided my every move, keeping me alive and providing me the strength to save everyone else. There be no other way to describe the unraveling of events other than a true miracle. The others put their trust in my actions and now I cannot ignore the urge to do the same for Samuel and Gregory. Perhaps Samuel will be granted the chance to explain our escape, telling of the unjust horrors we endured in the prison. A Reverend started the madness that has unfolded, so perhaps it shall take another Reverend to end it.

Regardless, our parents did nothing as their children suffered for months, my own Mother and Father cheerful at the confession of their dying son. The only wish I hold is to be cleared of witchcraft accusations and for the others to regain their innocence as well. A life spent in fear is not one that we desire.

Even if Gregory can return normalcy to Warren Hollow, what shall be the life we live? Returning to our homes, ignoring the cruelty of our parents and the murder of friends and family? Will they simply apologize and welcome us back? Perhaps we should hold little faith in resorption and continue the plan of traveling far away to create a life worth living.

"I want to have faith, Thomasin," I say as we begin to advance, "but can the damage truly be undone? How can we return to these homes, empty of our brothers and sisters?"

Robert comes forward and provides his thoughts as well. "That be true, Emelie. If somehow Gregory clears our names, I do not know if I can ever return to my parents for what they have done," he says.

To diminish the rising debate, I carefully provide more of my own thoughts. "Maybe Samuel will convince everyone of our innocence. And if Gregory acts upon his word, then we may have nothing to fear." I pause, attempting to cautiously explain both sides. "There be few of us left, and some may give in to temptation and rush home at the first opportunity. Still, many of us wish to never return to this place, traveling as far as we can."

Carefully I try to explain the horrors I faced while we make our way through the forest. I feel that it is my duty to inform everyone of my experiences to remain completely honest. I stop in my tracks, and suddenly all the others surround me with confusion.

'Tis time to tell the whole truth.

"When Thomas took me, I thought I walked to my death. Instead, he brought me home to my Mother and Father. Yet my home did not feel as though it was a home, and my parents did not seem like the parents of memory," I say.

I turn my attention forward and slowly start walking once more, not wanting to face the others as I continue my explanation.

"Rather than murder me quickly, Thomas wanted to torture me in the worst of ways. My brother confessed to witchcraft in order to save us, or as Thomas allowed him to believe. The younger children were starved and tortured just like us, and he was the only one left."

Some of the others cry out, now realizing that their brothers and sisters met the same fate. They have suspected such a tragedy from my earlier words, yet now it is spoken clearly and fully understood.

"Just before my brother passed, Thomas brought him and I to our home in order for me to confirm his cruelty. John agreed to take the blame and confess to welcoming bewitchment at the hands of Rose. He knew he would die, so he took the opportunity at hand to sacrifice himself for our freedom. John told Reverend Thomas that he and Rose conjured spirits and communicated with the Devil, and that All Hallows Eve was their night to bewitch the others," I explain.

Henry comes forward, angry and disgusted by the actions of Thomas. "But Thomas and your parents did not believe his words, did they?"

I shake my head. "Mother and Father believed, caring little for his death. They held excitement that John shall confess before death and have a chance to find redemption in heaven. But Thomas saw through the lies of a child, and he made that clear on the way back."

I fight to contain my emotions while discussing the unraveling of events.

"John spent his final moments in my arms. I provided him reassurance and thanked him for saving us. He needed to believe that his death was for our freedom, so I devised a plan to make that possible. We left my home, and that is when the Reverend began to mock John and revealed his true intentions. Regardless of my brother's words, we were never to be free. Thomas said we were to rot in the prison until spring, when he would murder us all," I say.

"And how did you convince the Reverend to enter your cell all alone?" Robert asks.

I pause before answering, peering at Thomasin who stands by my side. She notices my gaze and places her hand on my shoulder.

"I had to convince Thomas that there was a witch amongst us. It took plenty of effort but eventually I filled him with fear. Rather than acting rationally, he rushed to the prison on his own, ready to confront Thomasin as the true witch."

The others gasp in surprise, and I begin to crumble out of guilt.

"I apologize once more, Thomasin, please forgive my actions. 'Twas the only way I knew to get Thomas in a vulnerable position. He suspected that we wanted to escape so I needed to get him alone."

Thomasin stops walking and turns to face me. She understands my guilt and pulls me in for a tight embrace.

"I told thee I was the most powerful witch of all, but none would listen," Thomasin says jokingly. "Of course I forgive thee, you risked your life and nearly met death so that we could be free. And after what you did to Thomas I fear for my own safety if I disagree." Thomasin pulls away, hiding her neck with her hands. I let out a laugh, joyful that all is forgiven, and the truth has finally been revealed.

Our conversation has drifted my mind from the weather, which begins to slow once more. The snow calms and the sun begins to peek over the trees. We have survived through the night, and shortly we shall arrive at Rose's home where we can rest. Suddenly I feel anxious to reveal the final act that is needed once we arrive. "There be one more issue that needs attention," I say nervously, "Samuel was to assist me but now he is no longer with us."

I raise my hand and remove the covering; the others pull away at the very sight of it. "It is not without injury that I walked away from my encounter with Thomas. As you can tell, he tortured and nearly killed me. But the worst of all is that the weather took this hand. To save my arm, Samuel advised that my hand must be removed once we arrive."

The others stare at my hand, offering no replies to such a request. With my other hand I reach into my coat and reveal the blade that Samuel gifted me. "Samuel provided me with this knife, as the sharpness should make a clean cut. And I am sure that Rose would have other equipment to keep me alive after," I say with assurance.

After a few moments of silence, Henry boldly steps forward. He takes a closer look at my hand, and volunteers to help. Perhaps this is his chance to prove himself and win my favor once more.

"I think I can help you, Emelie. My Father taught me how to make the cleanest of cuts, as I often assisted him in animal preparation," Henry says.

Henry's Father is referred to as one of the greatest farmers and butchers in all of New England, when he is not a drunken fool of course. He provides services for all, often drawing in travelers from neighboring colonies for his talents. While a butcher would not hold the level of care and knowledge as a wet nurse, Henry may still possess the skills to safely remove my hand.

"Trust me, Emelie," Henry says with content, "I have seen similar injuries in some of our livestock. Your hand must be removed to save your arm, and I believe I am particularly skilled in culling."

"Thank you, Henry, although I am not an animal sent to the slaughter. Will I be safe when it is done?" I ask.

"Yes, the process should be rather simple. I am willing to do such a kindness for you after all you have done. Please find me once we arrive when you would like to begin."

I nod to Henry, appreciative of his offer but also fearful of the results. The realization that I shall lose my hands begins to instill heavy fear within me. However, I accepted that my hand would be the sacrifice of surviving on this day. After my encounter with Thomas, I am fortunate to still be breathing, so losing a hand appears as a fair price when many others have lost their lives.

Subtly I make my way to the front of our group once more. My wish is to remain alone and gather my thoughts as we walk the final stretch of our journey. All the contemplation and conversation among the group has allowed me to remain out of my head for the duration of our escape. Sometimes I do wish to be left alone with my thoughts, recalling details and constantly devising a strategy in my head.

The sun climbs higher in the sky and the storm has passed, bringing further ease among the group. Hope and positive feelings continue to build as we venture further and further from The Hollow. Although it is with difficulty to deny the battle we all face within, as everyone else must struggle with the same feelings as I. Deciding to move forward or returning to our homes after all is resolved, trusting Gregory to have the power to do so, wondering if Samuel is already dead, and grieving over lost friends and loved ones. Thankfully we have each other, or else I fear none of us would have survived all that we have gone through. They look to me for guidance and as a savior, but it was all within themselves to stay alive and believe in reaching an end. In honesty, I struggle to devise a plan for my own future. 'Twas simple to develop a plan for murder and escape from a prison, but what comes next is something that cannot be easily envisioned.

Will you go back to the village if the witch hunt ends, or shall you travel forward and reach the destination of your dreams? Were all those promises to John a lie if you surrender? You cannot hold anger towards the others who choose to go back to The Hollow, that urge grows in you as well no matter how hard you suppress it.

The thought of returning to Mother and Father fills me with disgust, yet for reasons unknown I cannot deny the pull of returning to my familiar surroundings. Beyond Warren Hollow awaits a life of uncertainty and unknowns, though if we are to be forgiven and proven innocent then surely we could be welcomed back home. But

John is dead, like many others, and our parents were to celebrate at our execution if given the chance. This is a struggle I must hold in silence until the certainty of safety arises.

"Almost there," I say with positivity to disrupt the contemplation. Most of our travel beyond the village consists of inner struggle. Many are grieving at the truth that I have revealed to them, and now our encounter with Gregory has shifted the desires and plans of our future. Although the one certainty is that we all desperately need rest and a place to recover. The surroundings begin to look familiar, and I know we are close to Rose's home.

This is a path I have not walked for nearly a year or so, as my final venture to these woods came alongside Mother and John. It was a warm summer day, before any talk of witchcraft or the black arts. John wrapped himself around my back in his usual position, and Mother joined us as she often would to spend time with her dear friend, Rose. Upon arrival, I would look through the many books and scrolls that Rose gathered over the years while they tended to my brother. We visited so often that she be the reason I and many of the other children can read. Rose would often feed John healing herbs and berries, using ointments on his legs and engaging in various practices to ensure his continued health. Mother could never thank Rose enough, labeling her as the sole reason my brother survived his birth and continuously overcame his ailments. Rose received the utmost respect from nearly everyone in Warren Hollow and was a friend to all. She would spend hours discussing the offerings of nature and which berries were safe to eat or what plants could be used for healing. After church service she would make playful jest of the scoldings that some children would receive for sinful behavior, and always kept the secrets of desires we concealed from our parents. She was never present in the church herself, respectfully showing no interest in faith or the teachings of a Reverend.

Our true bonding came when she began to organize bonfires in the forest. What once started as a small secret quickly reached the magnitude of our All Hallows Eve celebration. Even with growing suspicion, she continued to provide frolic for us until the day of her imprisonment. Rose had a playful nature, and she understood the yearning for freedom that all the children shared. Rather than scold us like our parents or church officials, she emphasized the importance of embracing freedom and individual thinking.

I have always looked to Rose as a friend, but now I see how much of an impact she has had on my life. After all that has happened, Rose shall assist us children one final time after death.

"I see it!" Thomasin yells.

I turn my gaze in her direction, and our destination is within view. The others shout with joy as we begin to hasten our steps. We now stand just outside of Rose's home. It appears to be unharmed, aside from a large cross painted on the door. With little effort I force the door open, and the others follow close behind.

All of us stand on the inside, out of the cold and away from The Hollow. The others begin to walk around the home and study their surroundings. Nearly everything looks accurate to my memory, yet a sadness fills the air. All the plants and flowers lay dead across the floor and windows. It appears there was a struggle, as a few bowls and glass cups lay scattered across the floor. Many of the supplies remain in place, countless jars full of healing remedies and flowers carefully preserved. A shelf full of books and writings nearly reaches the ceiling, and out of curiosity I venture into unfamiliar areas of the home. Thomasin stays close to my side as we wander into Rose's cellar.

Light shines through a small window, illuminating the contents of the room. For a moment I am taken back to a memory in our cell, as this room is eerily similar. Thomasin senses my growing agitation so she walks closer and places her head on my shoulder.

"I am sorry, Thomasin...sorry for all of it," I cry out. Once more the emotion becomes too difficult to bear and tears fall down my face. "If Thomas had killed you then I would be at fault."

"I told thee many times, you are forgiven," Thomasin says reassuringly. "And I did not die today, because of you I am here with all our friends. Thomas is dead and we are free. You mustn't blame yourself for the death of others. What could you have done while locked in a cell? When the time arose, you ensured our freedom unlike anyone else."

Thomasin begins to search the room while continuing her explanation, rummaging through boxes and jars. "Ezekiel and the others acted in anger, which cost them their lives. Even Rose chose not to act and surrender when given the chance. And this is why the others looked to you for guidance. You watched your brother die, yet you remained calm and outsmarted the most evil being in The Hollow. Your intelligence and instinct of survival is why we are here," Thomasin says.

I appreciate her words and reassurance. Slowly I walk over to Thomasin, joining her in the search through Rose's belongings. The frigid temperature causes icicles to form over the window just as in our cell. We recognize that the cellar holds nothing of importance, so it is time to rejoin the others in the warmth of the upstairs. Sure enough, our friends have unpacked the few belongings that were stolen from the courthouse. William struggles to maintain a small fire while Robert and the others count the rations of food and clothes in our possession.

"Emelie, Thomasin!" A voice calls from the kitchen. I recognize the voice to be Catherine, a young child of The Hollow I have yet to create a bond with. We walk into the kitchen and spot Catherine, Mary, and Edith, a group of girls who were too old of age to join their friends in the other confinement, but still quite younger than the rest of us.

"Come, let us clean thee," Mary exclaims happily. The girls have prepared cloths and some healing herbs in a bowl of water. Mary and Edith are twin sisters, who also spent plenty of time with Rose before her execution. She taught many of the younger children how to understand nature and simple practices, just as she has done for me at a young age. Catherine may not share the blood of the sisters, yet she is undoubtedly one of them. I recall Father speaking of an unfortunate illness that took Catherine's Mother and Father, leaving her in the care of Mary and Edith's family. Regardless, younger children always shared even a closer bond of friendship than the likes of us older children.

These are good children, undeserving of the torture we have endured. I know for certain none of the three were present at any of our forest bonfires.

To please them, I push my thoughts of pity and remorse aside and smile. "Hello girls, are you to make us look delightful?" Thomasin asks.

The girls motion tactfully for Thomasin and I to sit. We join them in chairs and immediately the girls start to cleanse our bodies. They wet our hair and begin to scrub our faces and necks to wash away the filth. I catch a glimpse of my appearance in the reflection of the water bowl. My hair is in tangles, blood dried across my head and the entirety of my face swollen beyond recognition. One of the girls breaks my stare by splashing Thomasin and I with the water. I let out a laugh, thankful for the joyful relief from my own sorrow.

Over the next few minutes, the girls take their time washing our hair and bringing life back to us. I watch as the water drips from my head, collecting blood and turning the bowl unpleasant shades of red. The girls pay no mind to the horrific site of my injuries, instead they make jokes and talk of boys and the time they spent with Rose. Thomasin and I quickly meet each other's gaze with a smile, as these girls remind us so much of ourselves when we were of a younger age.

Thomasin often spent her days chasing after boys and causing playful chaos among the others, yet my focus at that age was unadorned until the day of our capture. Spending time in the forest was the only happiness I needed in my life. Something about nature always called to me much louder than engaging with the other children. Perhaps John, Thomasin, and Rose were the only other people who understood me, and I am thankful to still have Thomasin by my side. I could not have endured this situation without my greatest friend.

Henry eventually makes his way into the kitchen. His presence interrupts the laughter and sends a shock through my body. I have forgotten about what must be done with my hand. Henry stares at me, trying his best to fake a smile for the children. I notice that he takes a few glances at my hand, which is now curled up tightly in my lap. I nod to Henry, letting him know that I am ready for his assistance. He notices my signal and takes his leave from the room. The moment I have dreaded with each passing minute has come. Adrenaline fills my body and I let out a long exhale. Slowly I begin to stand, Thomasin starting to join me as well. "No," I tell her as I gently signal her back into her chair, "these girls have much work left to do before you can face the others."

Nervously I joke with Thomasin to let her know I will be alright, but she does not laugh like the younger girls. Still, she understands my desire to go through this without an audience, so she submissively drops back to her chair.

"Are you certain?" She asks. I nod, smiling back and preparing to exit the room. Immediately the girls begin to continue their work, brushing and drying Thomasin's hair without any care. She and I share one final moment of connection through our gaze, and I cannot delay the inevitable any longer. My body begins to motion towards the exit of the kitchen and into the area with the others.

Passing through the doorway, a warm gust of wind and the smell of smoke hits my face. William has successfully started a blazing fire in the hearth. The others prepare food and water in pots to boil over the flames. Everyone is so distracted by our current surroundings that they pay no mind to my arrival. I feel relieved at my underwhelming entrance, as the mutilation that awaits is not something I want to draw any attention. Panning the room, I eventually spot Henry who awaits near the stairs. He does not take his eyes from mine, so I begin to walk in his direction. Passing through, I gently smile at the others who acknowledge my improved appearance. It does feel much better to have the blood wiped from my skin and to have taken a partial bath.

Henry appears nervous as I grow closer, and I cannot deny my feelings of anxiousness as well. We now stand face to face, and Henry struggles to maintain his composure.

"Everything is ready upstairs, Emelie, would you like to get this over with?" He asks.

I maintain my gaze, attempting to conceal my fear as much as possible. In truth I hope that my panicked demeanor is less noticeable than Henry's, who shares the look of Reverend Thomas when he entered our cell.

"Yes, Henry, let us be done with it," I reply.

Henry begins to climb the stairs and I follow. As we reach the top, all the commotion downstairs begins to fade into a powerful silence. I smile at the realization that all the commotion was a facade to ease my emotions. The focus of everyone's attention has never left me. While I appreciate their efforts and care, I simply wish to disappear back into a nobody among the crowd, especially at this moment. My heartbeat grows in intensity and my body begins to shake, as I know it is finally time to lose my hand.

XVIII

Take My Hand

The realization of still breathing is but a true miracle. Over the past few hours my body has taken an implausible amount of damage. Reverend Thomas's brutality has left me hanging onto life in a pool of my own blood, more than once since I was pulled from my cell. Hours spent in the snow damaged my skin and completely crippled my right hand. Vicious blows to my head have taken my consciousness as well, and for a moment in the prison the afterlife had its grip on me. Yet somehow I remain on this earth, perhaps through my determination to honor John or the power of God. 'Tis truly a miracle, and now this final moment of dread awaits.

Dear God, please grant me one final miracle through what I must endure. You have answered my prayers and guided my actions all through the night. And now one final time, I beg for my survival through this mutilation.

Henry leads the way, guiding the path to what used to be Rose's bedroom. He pushes open the door to reveal a collection of tools and contraptions. Two chairs sit facing each other in the corner of the room by the window. A dimly lit lantern illuminates flames on the walls, along with the sunlight fighting to creep in. "Sit please, it is best not to wait much longer," Henry instructs. "This will help with the pain."

Henry hands me some herbs and roots that Rose must have preserved. Without any thought I eat the herbs, fighting through the bitterness and foul taste with each mouthful. My curiosity overcomes me, and I begin to question Henry.

"Tell me, Henry…," I begin, "tell me what exactly will be done. Do not spare any details."

Henry shuffles with his tools and slowly turns in my direction. He wishes to hold back, yet I force him to explain.

"Father always followed the same process, regardless of the size or condition of the animal on the farm. First," he holds up Reverend Thomas's blade, "I will use this to make a clean and powerful cut. It is my hope that the first cut severs the hand, and if not the second surely will. After the hand is detached, I will then use this," he holds up a saw-like tool with rigid teeth, "this object shall evenly remove any muscle or bone left exposed."

I try my hardest to fight back tears as my lips begin to quiver. Slowly I struggle to raise my hand into view, taking a moment to stare at the mess that it has become. Total focus and strength still do not move my fingers in the slightest of motions, so I understand that it is time for it to be removed. Henry rolls up my sleeve further, revealing that the frostbite has climbed beyond my wrist. He studies my entire arm before touching just below my elbow.

"Here," he says while taking a closer look, "I must fasten this cloth tightly around this area. Everything below this must be removed."

Out of curiosity I ask why the cloth must be tied so tightly as he fastens it in place. "Father says to ligate the area to slow the bleeding," he replies.

"And what is to be done if the bleeding does not slow, Henry?" I ask nervously.

He pauses, doubting himself before giving me the last piece

of information. "Some of the animals die, Emelie. The sheer trauma or loss of blood has killed many on our farm who cannot bear it, yet Father has introduced a new practice that has nearly stopped all death. The pain shall be excruciating, but if I cannot slow the blood, would you like me to do what is necessary?" He asks.

I sit in silence, absorbing the gruesome details of what is to become of me. "Yes," I reply without further words, no longer wanting to know what the last resort to save my life shall be.

"Very well," Henry says.

He organizes the tools one final time before fastening the cloth on my arm even tighter. I wince at the tightness, feeling as though my arm shall fall off before he introduces any objects. Perhaps it is the start of the herbs overtaking me or staring death in the face once more, regardless I uncover some bravery and begin to question Henry on a much lighter subject.

"And tell me, Henry, how long have you had such a fondness for me?" I ask.

He stops dead in his tracks. To maintain his composure, he quickly rustles around with the tools, a desperate act to hide his own embarrassment or emotions.

"Henry," I say sternly to gather his attention.

He looks directly into my eyes, and for the first time I truly see the affection he holds for me. Out of fear and uncertainty I tried to avoid such an encounter, but I feel that Henry deserves this moment of reassurance and honesty.

"For as long as I can remember, Emelie," he says. "Yet I never dared to act on it."

"What say you?" I ask.

"I am but nothing more than a drunken farmer's son, with

no wealth or skills outside of handling animals. A mindless brute in the eyes of everyone. I understand who I am, so I chose never to act and make a fool of myself."

"I wish you would have, Henry."

I stare at him, both of us now face to face in our chairs. Slowly I pull myself towards him. He anxiously looks around the room before settling his eyes directly on mine, now refusing to break his gaze as I draw closer.

Suddenly a bout of dizziness overcomes me. The herbs begin to take effect and my balance begins to slip and the walls start to circle around me. Henry notices my current state and helps me rise from the chair. He holds my left arm and carefully guides me to the bed. He speaks to me, but the words become inconceivable, so I do my best to adjust myself. Henry lies me on my back, leaving my right arm hanging from the side. He searches the room, and after a few moments he slides a commode under my arm to keep it in line with the bed. The emotions begin to overcome me in my current state, and tears begin to fall from my eyes. I cannot keep my solid demeanor due to my inebriation. Henry attempts to calm me down, ensuring my safety before touching a single tool. I fight to sit up in the bed, and I pull my arm back to my body to protect it.

The clamor certainly alerted the others and I notice footsteps approaching the door. "John?" I call out in confusion. Momentarily the door slowly opens, and Thomasin enters the room. "Oh Thomasin, I cannot do it!" I cry out as she makes her way to the bed.

Peacefully she climbs into the bed, pulling me into her arms. The room spins as I try to focus on her face. She stares back at me, fighting tears and attempting to provide comfort. "Do not fear, Emelie, I am here, and Henry shall take care of you," she explains.

"And what if I am to die? I promised John that I would survive and lead us to freedom."

Thomasin slowly lays me back down on the bed. She places a pillow below my head and stretches my arm away from my body. I sob faintly but do not resist her movements. The herbs overpower my hearing as Thomasin's words become nearly inaudible.

"You shall not die. Henry knows what is to be done and I will stay by your side. I promise that you shall live beyond this moment. I love thee, Emelie, like a sister so deeply."

Thomasin grabs my left hand and pulls it into her own. Henry now stands above me on the side of the bed, and I know he anxiously wishes to begin. Thomasin turns my face towards her so that I do not watch as Henry prepares. With all my consciousness I ask one final request.

"Thomasin? If you are still in this room, please cover my mouth. I do not wish for the others to hear my screams," I request.

Forcefully I close my eyes, feeling Thomasin obey by gently placing her free hand over my mouth to silence the coming screams. After a few moments I feel the cold touch of the blade on my left arm. Henry searches for the exact spot to make his cut, moving the blade up and down my skin. Thomasin pulls me closer and whispers in my ear.

"You are the strongest person I know."

Immediately my eyes burst open, and I let out a scream as Henry plunges the knife through my arm. No amount of herbs or apothecary practices could have prepared me for the pain of which I endure. It's as though I feel every muscle and bone ripping and breaking under the force of the blade. Even in my intoxication I succumb to the pain behind losing a limb. I was immensely incorrect in assuming that the current state of my hand would have prevented any agony. The sounds of my own flesh tearing fills the room, forcing Thomasin to look away while still trying to cover my mouth the best she can. The pain forces me to wail intensely, with enough force that my head feels as though it may explode. Thomasin now restrains me on the bed, trying her best to calm my movements and allow Henry to continue.

Once more I feel the blade strike again, and I hear it penetrating straight through into the commode. True to his word, Henry has removed the better part of my arm in two attempts. I lie in a daze, pouring sweat and fighting to hold my consciousness. With a pathetic effort, I attempt to turn my head and observe Henry as he continues. Thomasin notices my movements and uses her hand to pull my face towards her again. She pushes her forehead into mine, blocking my sight and providing comfort in this horrific situation.

Time begins to stand still as I faintly recall Henry's words. *"This object will remove any remaining muscle or bone."* I remember the sight of Henry raising the saw-like tool and immediately I burst into a panic once more, fighting free from Thomasin's grasp.

"Thomasin! I am dying! I simply cannot bear anymore!"

Thomasin holds my body still while she signals for Henry to continue. "You are almost done, Emelie. The worst of such suffering is over," she says. I notice tears in her eyes as well.

My body temperature rises as I feel sweat pouring from my skin. The room begins to dim, and I fear that my consciousness finally escapes me. I watch Thomasin's face as it begins to fade into blackness. The only sound that fills my ears is of Henry's saw. I hear the motions as it moves back and forth, reminding me of the times assisting Father with the firewood. Pain is no longer an issue as my entire body has gone numb. My eyes do not fight to stay open, and the sound of the sawing is interrupted by a loud crash to the floor. Henry has successfully cleaved the bone and muscle, as he said would be a necessary step. The worst is over and now I can fall into this deep darkness of unconsciousness.

Over the next few moments, I hear rushing around the room, followed by the panicked voices of Henry and Thomasin.

"I feared this outcome, Thomasin! She bleeds too heavily!" Henry shouts in panic.

"What am I to do, Henry? She is going to die," Thomasin says emotionally.

Still my eyes remain closed, I lay unbothered by the voices and commotion that surround me. All pain has left my being as I start to drift into a desired sleep. The beating of my heart drastically slows to a steady pace with each passing second. Coldness fills the room, like the nights we laid frozen in the prison.

"Come with me in haste, Thomasin, we must follow through with the only option to save her," Henry instructs.

Thomasin cries out as she rushes behind Henry through the door. Before her exit I believe she shouted demands for me to hold on, yet I could not determine the words in full.

I would like to stay, Thomasin, but I am so cold and tired that I must go where my consciousness takes me. Perhaps I shall only rest my eyes for a few moments. It would be much easier without the sound of rushing water near the bed.

With all my strength I open my eyes enough to see if rain has found its way through the window, or if Henry spilled his bowl of clean water on the way out. I turn my head, only holding enough energy to fully open one of my eyes. As I look to the corner of the room, I realize that no windows are open, and nothing has spilled. The sound that prevents my sleep is the pouring of blood from my arm as it hits the floor. Sure enough, Henry has removed my hand, but his hopes of little blood flow have failed. I watch as blood flies from the open wound, nearly in a pattern with the slowing beat of my heart.

Henry bursts through the door with Thomasin close behind.

"She is still alive," he says frantically, "you must hold her arm out, Thomasin!"

Without hesitation Thomasin obeys, rushing to the side of the bed and holding what is left of my arm for Henry. I make no effort to dispute or speak, for the energy required is long gone. Henry follows behind, nearly slipping on my blood that coats the floor. Immediately I realize his intentions after spotting what he holds in his hands. Rather than watching, I close my eyes once more. Cautery was the final solution Henry had to keep me alive, and he takes position to begin.

Henry has the pot that was boiling over the fire, the bottom as bright and hot as the sun. Thomasin uses both hands to force my arm straight out for Henry, who slams the bottom of the pot against my wound. Suddenly a rush of adrenaline flows through my body, and I let out a scream so loud that I can taste the blood as wounds in my throat open from such force. The pot squeals as it touches my skin, undoubtedly saving my life.

XIX

Together

Winter's reign has come to an end and the warmth of spring engulfs the forest. Flowers return from the ground and leaves sprout from the trees and brush. Each day grows longer than the last with the sun hanging into the sky, well into the evening hours with each passing day. Sunshine radiates through the air, all signs of winter retreating until the year of next. Farming season shall soon return with vegetation breathing life once more. 'Twas a difficult winter, much more difficult than the last, but here we stand on the verge of a beautiful spring.

Months have passed since the night we arrived at Rose's wonderful home. I fought to stay alive for days after that horrid night, battling infection and slowly regaining my health, while adapting to life with one hand. The support of the others is what keeps me going. Thomasin has taken charge of the other girls, guiding the meals and making repairs to our shelter. They brought many of the plants back to life that miraculously survived the winter and kept us clean through bathing and techniques from Rose's books. William leads the boys on hunting expeditions and weekly scavenges for food. If God blesses our hunt with animals, then Henry prepares food for us as he has learned on his family's farm. If not, then we make do with berries and any plants that will not cause harm. Most importantly, we survived and continue to survive each day. The winter brought much starvation and sickness since that night, yet we have a shelter and the support of one another. Some remain faithful, reciting the prayers that have guided them through survival in the prison. I cannot deny my occasional prayer as well, for it was a true miracle by God that led us to this moment.

Robert has dedicated much of his time to scouting the village. Often, he will spend hours traveling back to The Hollow and watching for anyone that searches for our whereabouts. Not a single soul has left the walls throughout the entirety of winter. No signs indicate the success or failure of Samuel and Gregory, so we have found no reason to abandon Rose's home. There has been much discussion about venturing further, but we often agree to remain in place for a little while longer. Days pass without a single word of witchcraft or discussion of the events we have endured. We are all living in the present, perhaps wanting to forget what caused such a situation and pretending this be a normal life.

A full winter spent in this home has made us a family. We survived because of the bravery and sacrifices of those no longer with us. I find myself ashamed and guilty as days pass when thoughts of John do not fill my mind. This is a life he would have deeply enjoyed, as this is the paradise I aimed to reach with him. It feels immoral to walk through the forest or enjoy one second of our freedom, because it was his loss of life that granted me such peace. Most of the others struggle in silence as well, yet together they have returned to good health and hold positive spirits.

"Emelie, I see you rise to wake before the sun on this beautiful day," Thomasin says as she approaches. She joins me in sitting by the stream. Often, I wake before the others to clean their clothes in the water and enjoy the beautiful weather.

"Good morning, Thomasin, was but Henry's snoring that caused me to flee from that house," I reply playfully. Thomasin laughs as she begins to pull the clothes from my basket.

"I can do this, for I adapt better by the day," I say, prideful with slight embarrassment.

Since losing my hand, Thomasin has assisted me each day in learning to adjust and live a normal life. It has not been without difficulty, and her persistence can cause embarrassment at times, but her intentions are pure so I let her help without dispute.

"It takes two hands to fold clothes, Emelie, so unless you intend to grow another then it looks as though I am stuck to your side," she says.

I laugh at her inappropriate humor, splashing water from the stream onto her face. One thing that has not died during the winter is our friendship. We have been through pain and suffering together, and here we remain, side by side.

"Do you remember when we washed up in the stream before All Hallows Eve?" I ask Thomasin. Recalling such events feels as though I refer to another life or memories that are not my own. While that was less than a year ago, we are no longer the same people that we were on that day.

"Aye, 'tis true I think of that day quite often. Ezekiel presenting his wild ideas of celebration, and the two of us complaining about our parents making us prisoners in our homes. If only we had known…"

"But Ezekiel did speak a convincing tale. He always found a way to make us break the rules and brought excitement to our lives. He was quite courageous, but also an idiot!"

We laugh and relish in the memories of our friends no longer with us. Ezekiel was a fool in fact, but he cared for us and was never afraid to confront our parents or any who treated us poorly. His presence is greatly missed among our group every day.

"Henry practically begged me to assure your attendance, Emelie. Once you came by and told us that you changed your mind, he planned on finally taking action that night in the forest. Although it took some convincing for him to find the confidence," Thomasin says.

Her words catch me by surprise, as I am now fully aware that a quick goodbye to Henry was to be much more. I recall my nervousness, but also the excitement that I felt in that moment, just before the attack began.

"We have had our moments," I say, "but he has yet to act any further."

"Then you must wait no longer and act yourself," Thomasin says as she splashes me with water.

I fold the last of the clothes to the best of my ability, and Thomasin rushes to carry the basket back to Rose's home. We begin to make our way through the trees, walking slow to enjoy the rising sun and the beautiful weather.

"Did you ever imagine we would stand where we are today?" Thomasin asks.

"Aye, 'twas never any other option for us. Some of those nights I feared that death stood close by, but I kept telling myself that I needed to save John," I reply.

Thomasin shows sorrow for my words, now focusing her attention forward as we continue walking.

"When John died in my arms, I simply wanted to give up. Yet, his death could not go unanswered. I promised him that we would break free and live the life we desired."

"In the prison, just after you killed Thomas, I thought that you had died, Emelie. We all did," Thomasin says.

"Perhaps for a moment I did leave this earth. But it was not my time, and I needed to come back and save the others."

"Did…," Thomasin struggles to ask, "did you wish to die after rescuing us?"

While I wish to speak it not, I realize that she deserves the truth. Thomasin should know what was racing through my mind on that day.

"Yes, Thomasin. Perhaps I felt that I only deserved to live long enough to free the others because I could not save my brother. Or perhaps I merely wanted revenge. I let Thomas abuse me and risked everything so that I could fulfill what I believed was my purpose. If I did not wake up from the floor of the prison, then I felt that my contributions were done, and that would have been a most desirable ending. But God had a different plan."

We spend the next few moments walking in silence. Rose's home comes back into view as we continue on the dirt path. For the first time I feel as though I have spoken my honest thoughts out loud, giving someone else a look into the depths of my mind. While my words may be difficult to hear and not the typical expectations of a selected leader, they are real and true.

"If it makes you feel any better, Emelie," Thomasin begins once more, "I am glad that you are here with us. Because of you we are free, and I want you to know that your life still has purpose. You are my dearest friend, and I am happy that you did not give your life to be a martyr," Thomasin says as she smiles at me.

"In truth, Thomasin, I am as well," I reply.

As time passes my thoughts on death and my true purpose begin to shift. I spent months plotting an escape from the walls of the prison, and after John died, I felt that my death should follow.

My plan almost worked, I executed Thomas and the others gained freedom, so my desires were achieved. But I was brought back to this earth, perhaps God has more plans for my future and death was not my destiny on that night. It may have been a hallucination or a true vision from the other side, but my final meeting with John provided me the closure I needed to survive. And that experience brings me peace and fulfillment. The truth was spoken to Thomasin, as I truly am grateful to live and achieve the wishes of Rose and John.

We arrive back to Rose's home and a few of the others make their way outside, starting the day by relaxing on the stairs while Catherine and her friends engage in frolic. Robert tends to the flowers with his tools while Henry struggles to open the windows. Everyone does as they desire, making contributions and focusing on fun and freedom. Not a moment of conflict or disagreement has ever transpired among our group. We live in the future that we longed for while behind those walls. Many of the others in the prison would talk of doing as they please every day and what they could contribute if we were lucky enough to gain freedom. Today is a fine example of the truth behind our words, as we are a group of survivors who set a goal and achieved it. Now we live day to day, doing what we can and waiting for the future to decide what is next.

Robert opens the door for Thomasin and I upon our return. We thank him and make our way inside, greeting the others who prepare for the day with breakfast, and laughing at the others still sleeping soundly.

"Will you make your way to The Hollow today, Robert?" I ask curiously. He shrugs his shoulders, indicating that he is unsure if that will be necessary.

"I make the journey and stare at walls that never open.

Perhaps they have forgotten about us, or perhaps they have all killed each other by now," Robert replies.

"That would not be of surprise," Thomasin adds.

"Even so, today is a beautiful day. I do not mind making the walk back there. And if nothing comes of it, then maybe I shall stop watching any longer," Robert says.

"That seems reasonable, thank thee for one final day spent watching that place," I reply sincerely.

Robert gathers his belongings to venture back on one final retreat. Some of the others have joined him throughout the winter and early spring, but I never felt any desire to see The Hollow ever again. The unfolding of events and the tragedy within those walls is something I would like to remain in the past.

I leave Thomasin's side to return the clean rags to the kitchen. Henry prepares today's meal for us like he does day after day.

"Good morning, Emelie, would thy care to help skin these squirrels?" He asks.

I laugh, declining his offer and placing the clean garments in their designated places.

"William and a few of the others are said to have spotted a large deer roaming the woods. We would surely go to sleep much more brimful compared to when we eat these squirrels and rodents," Henry says.

"Certainly, yet I am grateful we no longer starve and all receive fair portions. We are truly thankful for thy skills in preparing these provisions," I reply.

I watch as Henry uses knives and other objects to turn a lifeless animal into what will be tonight's supper. Momentarily I am taken back to the night he removed my hand. Without any doubts I would have died if Henry did not act quickly and forcefully stop the bleeding with the burning pot. He understands my gratitude and makes little fuss over his heroic actions. I have noticed that he feels guilt when we are together or discussing my hand, and he hasn't dared mention our talk of affection. The brutality and complications that arose on that night could have cost my life, but I reassure him that there was no other option. Maybe Samuel would have removed my hand in a more delicate and educated manner, but his departure left little options with my rapidly declining health.

Now that I have greeted the others and completed my morning contributions, I seek a private space to recline. Often, I will spend time in Rose's bochord, a room she dedicated to organizing her countless books and writings. Hours go by as I deeply dive in the recipes and teachings within those collections. My knowledge on healing and apothecary practices has grown tremendously throughout our time in Rose's home.

Like most days, I make my way to the room and gently close the door. I have spent time studying a tome that Rose has worked on herself. We were unaware that Rose began documenting her practices, as she has filled many pages with simple recipes and techniques for healing. This collection does not have a name or a direct purpose, but she gives details on herbs and how to accurately make brews and ointments. Unfortunately, her capture prevented documentation of any further knowledge, so I find myself reading the same passages over and over.

Rose was a guiding figure to all of us. She did everything in her power to keep my brother alive after his birth and allowed us all to see the world for what it is, away from any unjust scoldings or teachings in the church. Our parents and the officials of Warren

Hollow were undeserving of her services, and her death shall never be justified. This space of Rose's home allows me to venture through my thoughts, like my actions in the prison. Yet, I no longer drive myself to insanity. Instead, I reminisce on the past and recall wonderful memories with Rose and my brother. Sometimes I read, or sometimes I simply place my head on the desk and drift off to a quick slumber while reliving vivid memories in my mind.

A noise from outside the door awakens me, as I have fallen asleep in my reminiscence. Perhaps I was asleep for a few hours, so I stand up and return the books to their shelves. As I struggle to place the final book back on its highest shelf, the door suddenly swings open before me. Mary and Edith rush to me and catch me by utter surprise.

"What is wrong?" I yell.

"Come quickly, Emelie, Robert has returned in a panic," Edith replies.

Quickly they leave the room, and without hesitation I follow. We move briskly through the hall and out into the main living area of the home. All the others have gathered a circle around Robert, who appears breathless and fearful.

"Please allow me to explain," Robert begins. He struggles to keep his composure, showing signs that he ran back from the village.

"I was watching the gates of The Hollow as I do most days. Suddenly they opened, and I watched as two men emerged from inside. They did not spot me, but they moved in haste, precisely in this direction. I ran as fast as I could, but I fear they are not far behind!"

Commotion erupts, as the others shout and move frantically around the home. The younger children crawl out of sight and hold each other in tears. Thomasin lays her eyes on me and rushes to my side.

"What are we to do?" She asks in a panic.

I stare at everyone for a few moments as if I am frozen in time, watching as they panic and rush around the room. Immediately I am taken back to our time in the prison and the chaos of our escape.

"I am not sure, Thomasin," I say.

She is visibly not satisfied with my answer as she attempts to find a solution. "You need to do something, Emelie, they will listen to you!" She yells.

For the first time in months, I am asked to reclaim leadership over the group. Since the night of our escape, I have attempted to hide on the outside and away from attention. In this moment I wish to join the younger children and hide on the floor. No longer do I want to lead or give direction. But I understand Thomasin's words, and there is no time to cower or allow further panic. Without hesitation I climb onto a chair, Thomasin holds my legs as I struggle to keep my balance. Henry notices my actions and shouts at the others to become silent and listen. Everyone stops moving and their eyes all land upon me. Admittedly I become uncomfortable, not wanting to once again decide our next move. Losing my hand has stripped my confidence, and I wish to never have anyone look at me. Nervously I hide my arm behind my back, feeling pathetic and anxious. Yet, I look at everyone's faces and know that I must quickly offer a solution.

"Robert, are you certain there were only two of them?" I ask.

"Yes," Robert says as he walks forward, "presumably two men coming in our direction. They wore clerical clothing, yet I could not clearly identify who it be."

"Thank you, Robert," I reply, remaining calm to relax the others. We only have a few moments to prepare for their arrival if Robert's words be true.

How did these men discover our location? Perhaps they have known of our whereabouts this entire time, and now they aim to recapture us once more. Or maybe they tortured Samuel into exposing us.

"If there only be two of them, then perhaps they do not aim to capture us or launch an attack. Surely they would bring plenty of others, armed and prepared as they were on All Hallows Eve," I say.

Carefully I climb down from the chair and make my way to the door. "It would be unwise to plot an escape right now. They are moments away and we would be unable to gather what we would need to leave this place."

"Then what are we to do, Emelie? I do not want to go back to that prison!" Edith cries.

The younger children are scared, but admittedly the rest of us cannot hide our fear either. Our quiet life will be interrupted once more. Perhaps we should have kept moving, or prepared for the day that they would come to take us. Alas, such a day has arrived, and we are left with little options. I begin explaining the only reasonable solution I can conjure.

"I see only one solution to this visit. We must cooperate and listen to what they come to tell us," I say.

Some argue that we must flee while others continue gathering supplies in a panic. "They cannot force us to go if there only be two of them. If they try then we will refuse, so there is no need to worry. When they arrive, I will go out to face them alone," I explain.

"No, you do not know what they want with us!" Henry yells. Thomasin makes her way to me, supporting the words of the others who dispute my actions. "If there are two of them," Thomasin begins, "then it only makes sense for two of us to meet them. Please, Emelie, allow me to do this with you."

Thomasin pleads to assist me, and perhaps that would ease the group even more. I agree but instruct everyone to wait on the other side of the door.

We continue gathering supplies in the following moments. The back door to Rose's home has been held open so the others can make an escape if necessary.

"Here," Henry says as he gives Thomasin and I knives to conceal, "just to be sure."

We accept the weapons and hide them within our clothing. The others gather around to console us and help us prepare for the arrival, which should be any moment. Reluctantly Thomasin and I make our way to the outside and securely close the door behind us. I let out a deep breath, gathering myself after assuming such a role once more.

XX

Cessation

For the next few moments, we stand outside of Rose's home in uncertainty. I turn to Thomasin who stares down the path, focused and ready for the disruption that soon approaches.

"Thomasin," I say in a serious tone, "becoming the leader was not my desire. 'Twas simply my wish to remain unnoticed, like before this madness. Nobody cared for my words back then, and in truth I did not mind. And how do they assume me to be a leader, for I am no better than anyone else? I only have one hand and wish to cower under such pressure."

"I understand, Emelie, but you have done wonderful things for us. You have acted with intelligence and somehow stayed calm when nobody else could," Thomasin replies.

"Aye, my only desire was to save my brother and return to the forest. And even before All Hallows Eve, I never wanted such attention."

For the first time I vocalize my true thoughts to my dearest friend. "While I always admired your presence and spending time with our friends, I only felt to be myself in the forest. I was never like them, yet you and Rose truly understood me. Mother and Father never held a grasp on my life either," I admit.

"I agree, the few of us were nothing but mere outsiders among the others. But Rose always recognized your potential and would speak as such to everyone. You are a very powerful presence, and your careful plotting and will for survival was recognized by the others. Robert was the village idiot and I was but a maker of mischief. But those roles have vanished. After what we have endured, we are all but family. And all of this was an opportunity for the others to recognize you," Thomasin says.

I stand in silence, understanding her words and accepting them as truth. Most of us were nothing before All Hallows Eve, as we did not need to be anything else but children. Perhaps my time with Rose has prepared me for such a situation, and the horrors that we have faced created a connection among all of us. Past roles held no value, and it just so happened that I was the best suited to guide the others through a tragedy. Before the witch trials I was nothing, yet this circumstance has given me purpose. Whether I wanted such power or not, the choice was never mine from the very beginning.

"There," Thomasin says as she points down the path. Sure enough, the two men emerge as they advance in our direction. I take a quick glance behind me, ensuring that all the others remain inside. They have obeyed our wishes, although their faces are pressed to the glass of nearly every window. The men notice us as well upon walking closer. They stop for a moment, and one of the men forces the other to remain in place. This man now approaches us alone while the other watches from a distance. Thomasin and I glance at each other, confused by their actions.

After a few moments the man makes his way to Rose's home, stopping as he stands a few steps in front of us. I recognize it to be Reverend Gregory, and suddenly I feel a wave of relief over my body. I lower my guard and relax at his presence. Gregory observes us and the home, then awkwardly raises his hand to wave at us.

"Hello to you both," Gregory says. "How great to see you

doing so well since our last conversation."

"Hello, Reverend, how did you find us?" I ask.

"Your dear friend Samuel guided my every step."

"Samuel!" Thomasin shouts, "Is he alive?"

Gregory smiles, appearing cheerful as though he brings nothing but good news. "Yes, Samuel is well. I promised nothing would happen to him on that night and I meant to keep my word," Gregory replies.

He begins to pace back and forth, seemingly anxious to provide the message that has brought him to us.

"We shall discuss Samuel soon, yet I hold information that I believe you would all like to hear. Would you ask the others to join us out here on this beautiful day?" He asks.

I notice Gregory takes a quick glance towards my hand, then looking away shamefully. In this instance, I refuse to hide it like I have done for months. Thomasin looks to me for guidance and I nod back, indicating that she can alert the others to join us. She turns to face the house, signaling for the others to come and listen to whatever Gregory must explain. One by one Henry, William, Robert, and all of the others make their way behind Thomasin and I. Gregory smiles at the sight of our group.

"It brings such joy to see you all, and I am so relieved that you have survived beyond that night," Gregory says.

"Not all of us," I reply as Gregory's smile fades at the realization of my words. "I suspect you are not visiting on this day only to wish us well."

"I come with much more than well wishes for all of you. Please listen attentively to my words children, as what I am about to say shall bring you peace," Gregory says.

The others anxiously draw closer, eager to hear what Gregory shall say next. We are nearly an hour's walk from The Hollow, so certainly he holds a message of importance.

"I promised you all that if I was given a chance on that night, through faith and good will, I would make things right in Warren Hollow. And I stand here today telling you that the witch hunt has come to an end, the nonsense of trials and accusations is over!" Gregory yells.

Thomasin covers her mouth in disbelief as tears begins to the flow. The others erupt in celebration and tears at Gregory's words as well, yet I remain motionless, and all sound begins to fade. I think back to the day of our capture, the months spent in confinement facing torture, and all the lives that were lost to such an irrational occurrence. Memories of John and I's final conversation crowd my mind, as it is hard to imagine we are free after a period of such hopelessness.

Thomasin forcefully pulls me into her arms, breaking me free from my thoughts and allowing me to express emotion like the others. I can no longer fight the plentiful feelings of sadness, joy, and relief that I have fought so hard to conceal since the very beginning. This is truly a special moment, one that will define the rest of our lives.

We all embrace each other, letting go of all the pain and finally recognizing true freedom. Gregory smiles at our reaction, allowing all the time we need before continuing his words.

"How is this so?" I ask Gregory as I regain my composure. The others halt their actions and listen to Gregory once more.

"The colony has adopted new methods within the courts. The cruelty and injustice that those accused of witchcraft have endured is now in the light. Foolishness of spectral evidence and hearsay from the mouths of accusers are no longer valid reasons to condemn the lives of the innocent. 'Twas nonsense from the onset, and this was prevalent long before the winter. What unraveled in Warren Hollow at the hands of Thomas should have never occurred, for this plague was ridden from most plantations before All Hallows Eve. Once word got out of such lunacy, I was one of the many forces sent to stop Thomas and restore order. Perhaps there be some dark-magic practicing witches out there, yet I have not seen one with my own eyes," Gregory explains.

"What is to come of us now? It is all simply over in an instant?" I ask.

"If you would return to Warren Hollow, the court wishes to reevaluate and pardon all suspected of witchcraft if cooperation is given. Once the formalities are covered, then you will soon be free once more. And this time I can assure fair practices and reasonable judgment," Gregory says.

Henry comes forward to continue questioning Gregory. "And what of our parents? Not so long ago they wished us dead at the hands of Thomas, and now they welcome us home as if nothing happened?" He asks.

Gregory loses his smile momentarily, understanding the adversity in Henry's question. When we met with Gregory in the courthouse, he explained that our village was in shambles. Parents and other adults were accusing each other, and The Hollow itself was falling apart.

"Through months of service and the arrival of new information, your parents look to do what is right. Faith guides them, and Thomas used that to gain power and convince them that he was acting as God intended. I have worked tirelessly alongside the court officials to banish the unjust teachings of Thomas. And I believe that we have found success. So long as you proceed through a trial of clearance, they wish to welcome you home and put an end to this nightmare," Gregory explains.

The others are unsure how to take such information, and I do not feel satisfied with Gregory's claims either. Perhaps he has restored some level of order to our home, but no amount of restoration could ever justify the lives taken or the torture endured. Neighboring plantations faced witch hunts and trials, and Reverend Thomas saw an opportunity to wreak havoc among us. This situation was never looked at through rational eyes, and not once did we have the chance to prove our innocence on such ridiculous claims.

"My brother lost his life, along with many others. They died without ever having the chance to prove their innocence," I say boldly.

Gregory takes a step closer as he begins to answer. "This is an unfortunate time, one that shall never be forgotten. But new laws develop by the day, allowing for an honest and appropriate process of conviction." Gregory weakens his act to speak honestly with us. "You children are a much different generation. Your parents live and die through faith, without ever questioning what they are given. But you all...you are all so untamed. I too am a man of faith in truth, but I see that perhaps there is free will for you all. 'Tis a struggle to bring the balance of faith and liberation to light. I try, sometimes failing and sometimes finding success," Gregory says.

We all absorb his words, accepting his truth and making our own assumptions. I do believe Gregory and his honest efforts within our village.

Even if we would not face execution upon entering through those walls, is that something we are willing to do? Can I face my parents, the ones who allowed my imprisonment and the death of my brother, and find forgiveness?

Gregory takes a few steps back and smiles at all of us once more. "I understand your confusion and frustration, and I welcome any criticism you may have. This message is not one you all were expecting, I am certain, yet I speak an honest truth."

To our surprise Gregory begins to walk away, making one final effort as he leaves. "There be no need to act on my words in haste. Today is a beautiful day, one to be enjoyed out here in the forest. Consider my words and act as you must. Yet I ask thee to come home at first of sunrise tomorrow, we all anxiously await your return to Warren Hollow," Gregory says.

He turns and walks away with a brisk pace. We are completely stunned by his visit, unable to properly react. Gregory makes his way to the companion who accompanied him on their journey. They speak for a moment, then Gregory continues walking back to the village as the other man starts to move in our direction. Our guard raises once more, anticipating the arrival of the next individual.

"Samuel!" A voice yells from behind me. Sure enough, it is Samuel who makes his way to our position. Thomasin rushes to embrace her dear friend as the others follow. Gregory kept his promise, and our friend did not lose his life as we feared. I notice that Samuel is dressed like Gregory, in the make of a clergy member. The others take turns greeting Samuel and exclaiming joy at his arrival. He lays eyes on me and begins to approach.

"Emelie, you are well," he says as we embrace, "I feared that your injuries would take you."

He pulls away to look at my hand, surprised to see that it was removed successfully and that I have survived.

"Henry kept me alive; he removed my hand that night and saved me. Everyone fought hard and we have lived here comfortably because of your sacrifice. 'Tis truly good to see you, Samuel," I say.

Our conversation gets interrupted as the others crowd around and suggest we all go back inside. We let our guard down and the tension vanishes once more. Samuel has returned to us, although I am wise enough to know that he comes with a purpose as well. We enter through the doors of Rose's home and the others drop their weapons and clear a space for everyone to gather. William provides Samuel with a drink as the others continue eating breakfast and return to their tasks. Curiosity overcomes me so I decide to break the jollification and ask of Samuel's intentions.

"Did Gregory send you here to convince us to return?" I ask as the room falls silent.

"No," Samuel says as he smiles at my question. "Gregory kept his word that night. I was fully prepared to give my life, yet he did not let that happen."

Samuel begins to walk around the room as he explains himself. "I was taken back to the prison; I spent a few more nights there without so much as a word from anyone. Then I was woken by Gregory, who took me directly to the court. Upon entering the courtroom, all our parents sat anxiously in attendance. Some showed fear at my presence, while others sat in silence, awaiting my words," Samuel says.

"You were given a trial?" I ask.

"Not exactly. The first thing asked of me was if I am bewitched. They did not ask me to confess, rather I was simply presented with that question. Before I answered, they asked if any of you were witches, and of course I told them no right away. At first it felt as though the only thing saving my life was that I knew of your whereabouts. They tried to get me to speak on it, yet I refused. Even now, Gregory is the only other member of The Hollow that finally knows of your hiding. None the less, I was informed that new rulings allowed me to explain myself justly, and that is exactly what I did. For what seemed like hours, I spoke the whole truth to everyone in the room. I told them of our fire and its innocence, and I spoke of Thomas's intentions and how he planned to execute us all unjustly."

"And how did they react to his murder?" I ask.

Samuel smiles as if he was waiting for someone to ask. "To my surprise," he begins, "I was not in the court on trial for witchcraft. Rather, they cared little after these initial words as if witchcraft was a thought of the past. Suddenly, our situation was approached with reason and civility. Perhaps the others thought it foolish for some time, but Thomas kept us in confinement fearing for our lives, unaware of this mindful shift. His murder was what brought me to the court. They wanted fine details of how I managed to murder the Reverend and free you all. I told them the version of the truth they needed to hear, the one Gregory and I felt necessary to convey. And this is the story of which they all believe." Samuel continues as we all keep close attention to his every word.

"Thomas brought Emelie back to the prison, holding onto life and beginning to slip away. He thought of me as her closest companion, so he ordered me to execute Emelie to traumatize everyone further. He unlocked my cell and exclaimed that Emelie would be the first of many to die by my hand. He instructed me to kill her, then to leave the prison and murder anyone who began to question his leadership. He gave me names that included officials and members of the church who recently arrived. In turn this would give me my freedom, but out of my good faith I turned the blade on

Thomas to save The Hollow. Once he was dead, I unlocked every cell and set you all free. You escaped quickly, but I was too weak to make it any further than that basement. That's where Gregory found me, ready to end my life as I begged for God's forgiveness," Samuel explains emotionally.

"And they believed you?" Thomasin asks.

"Yes," Samuel replies, "Gregory provided validation to my claims and the others did not question his words. He pleaded that I be taken into the church, rather than face execution or life in prison. No witch could speak the words of the Bible after committing such an act if God was not on their side. And that is precisely what happened. For my freedom, I have devoted my life to the church and follow in Gregory's teachings. 'Twas the only way."

That solves the mystery of why Samuel stands among us wearing the gown of a clergy member. He risked his life by staying in The Hollow that night, but he fulfilled his purpose and did what he felt was necessary. I can tell that he finds peace with his choice, perhaps moving on from the shame and guilt of surviving the night when the others died in the courthouse.

"Most people of our village aim to move on from these witch trials. Some still live in fear, but Gregory has found success in changing the public opinion. He is a much better Reverend than Thomas, and he understands the importance of fairness in court. They listen to him, and he has finally convinced everyone that you are all innocent, but they are still frightened. They must see for themselves that just like me, you are all innocent and human. Warren Hollow anxiously awaits your return tomorrow, and perhaps my intention is mere proof that there is truth and honesty in Gregory's claims," Samuel states in a convincing manner.

I know that Samuel would never lie to us. Perhaps Gregory

sent him here to convince us to return, but I do not see any trickery or ill intentions. Samuel feels that he and Gregory successfully restored a life at home for all of us. He begins making his way to the door. "I ask all of thee to consider these words. It may not be the same life as before, but there is still a life for you in our home," Samuel says as he prepares to exit Rose's home.

"Wait!" I yell, immediately as I rush to gather everyone's attention. Samuel turns around, waiting to hear my response before leaving.

"This will be our last night in Rose's home. Tomorrow everything shall change, but it is still today. And today I feel that there is one thing that must be done." I pause, grabbing Samuel's arm to convince him to stay. "Tonight, we shall have a bonfire. One large enough to reach the sky. And it would be a shame if you were not here for it, Samuel."

The others remain silent at my suggestion, perhaps feeling uncertain or shocked at such an idea. I stare at Samuel, nearly pleading with him to partake in this plan. Samuel smiles and walks back into the middle of the room.

"If we are to have such a bonfire, then we must begin gathering as much wood as we can!" He replies, giving in to my request. The others erupt with cheers at this final night we shall share together.

XXI

Full Circle

I t's as though All Hallows Eve is upon us once more. We have traveled back in time to a place where the only concern is gathering wood and celebrating. It seemed the only way to properly end our retreat would be with such an event. Soon after my suggestion I felt anxious, reasonably so after what happened the last time we held a bonfire. The past few months may have been prevented if there was no celebration on that night.

Even so, we did not get to rightly finish what we started. We wished to celebrate All Hallows Eve to the fullest, but that was the night our freedom was abruptly taken away. After months of death, suffering, and confinement, we shall reclaim our freedom in the very way it was taken. We waited patiently in Rose's home, surviving the winter and plotting our next move. The circumstances that brought us to our current shelter were not ideal, yet I believe some of the others have had the greatest time of their lives. All of us created a bond, finding our roles in ensuring safety and feeling appreciated for any contributions. Unspoken desires to become relevant and stand alone from a family name were easily achieved by all of us. Looking back at the past few months, we were able to live the way we always wanted for the first time. But tomorrow that will all change for each person here. There has been no discussion of Warren Hollow in the past few hours, and even though fear and uncertainty flow through each of our minds, we shall enjoy the night.

William and Henry prepare all the rations for a grand feast at the bonfire. Robert and Samuel gather the wood and clear a massive area to house such an event. Thomasin leads Catherine and the younger children in quickly creating decorations and making the area look wonderful. I have elected to spend these moments alone, taking one final time to admire Rose's library and scanning as many of her scriptures as possible.

Room by room I restore her home, cleaning each area to the best of my ability. Without this structure we all would have frozen to death in the snow. The foundation of our escape relied upon reaching this place, so I must show my respect. Rose was a beautiful person, so it is my wish to once more honor her friendship and life. Nervously I prepare a brief speech for tonight's bonfire. As I have confessed to Thomasin, being a leader was never a desire of mine. And now that my power will certainly dissolve tomorrow, I find it appropriate to make a parting statement and bid farewell to this role. Suggesting a bonfire was a risk, but one I felt appropriate and necessary. We have the opportunity to make things right and enter the future on our own terms.

I plan to honor all of our dear friends that we have lost, and to do so I have requested Thomasin and the girls create a memorial for those no longer with us. Most of the day has passed, so I watch the sun begin to dim in the sky. My work on the inside of Rose's home is complete, so I decide to escape through the backdoor to take a walk in the forest alone. Laughter and cheers fill the trees, indicating that our celebration shall soon begin. This makes me smile as I venture from the path. The air has the slightest chill, but it is a glorious spring night. Walking aimlessly for a few minutes, I ensure that I be far enough away from the others before taking a moment to rest. For the first time in months, I am surrounded by nothing other than blooming flowers and vegetation. While it is beautiful, I did not come out here to partake in admiring nature.

What am I to do?

A simple question that I ponder in my mind. The others have not spoken a word as to what they will do upon the sunrise. I suspect most of our group will return to The Hollow, going through the formalities and clearing their names of any witchcraft labels. The younger children will blindly walk into their homes, forgiving their parents and pretending as though nothing has happened. Yet I cannot blame them, I too put faith in Samuel and Gregory's words. Samuel would never lead us into the village if he did not believe in restoration himself. Once again, I am confronted by the fear of facing my parents. Mother had a smile on her face upon John's death, and Father remained weak. 'Tis challenging to determine what Thomasin shall do come sunrise. Those like Henry or Robert appear just as sickened by The Hollow as I, but the fear of an unknown future outside of those walls can be intimidating. I feel it is not my place to ask them or influence their choice, and I shall make that clear. Before pondering on their decisions, I must reach one of my own. The thought of returning to Warren Hollow and sitting in that church brings an ache to my stomach, but still, I sit here in contemplation. My brother died for this very moment, and having a choice is the hardest part of being free. Returning to the village is my choice, or venturing forward into a future of endless possibilities is my choice as well. While this is all we ever desired, I did not suspect the options would come with such tribulation.

This is why you never ventured any further, and always suggested staying stagnant. Whether you admit it or not, you held the desire of returning home just like everyone else. But what shall you do?

I battle with my thoughts, struggling significantly more to

reach a decision than anticipated. Rather than waste the night torturing myself, I simply wish to leave the forest and begin walking the path back to Rose's home. While the flowers and trees are beautiful, they have never given me advice or shown the same love that I give to them.

Suddenly I pause, feeling a wave of emotions overcome me as I leave the thickness of the forest. At this very moment I now realize that my true desires have changed. What was once the calling of the forest has been overthrown by a call to my friends. My happiest memories of the forest were with John, and rarely by myself. While I truly love being surrounded by nature, it was never the forest itself that called to me. Perhaps my feelings in the past were stronger, but after everything we have gone through, I now have a new devotion. Life in the forest, or anywhere else for that matter, will not be enjoyable without my friends. I spent night after night wishing to escape into nature, and now I understand that the forest was merely a cloak for my true yearning for freedom. These people are now my family, and all I desire is spending my life alongside them. If my friends wish to return to The Hollow, then so be it. I will walk through those gates and return to Mother and Father, so long as I get to be with Thomasin, Henry, and Samuel. If the sun rises and they traverse in the opposite direction, then I shall do so as well. They have given my life purpose and allowed me to uncover the feelings I have always concealed, my true self in honesty. So now I make my way back to Rose's home with a smile, feeling rejoiceful and fulfilled.

It could be argued that my faith has been fully restored. For the first time in months, I feel true happiness. I made a vow that I shall never turn my back to God after his guidance on that night. We have all learned to pray and accept faith in our own ways, not by the scolding words of a Reverend or as punishment from parents. Faith and scripture have taken on new meaning to all of us, and my faith has been restored in our future as well. All I ever desired was a choice, the ability to live the way I please at my own will. And that choice has finally come, but to my own surprise I gladly relinquish this freedom. 'Tis no longer just a decision of mine, for my friends will lead me on the path to whatever destiny they seek, and it shall become our destiny. Gladly I put all debate and contemplation aside as I approach Rose's home.

Smoke grows apparent in the air as I make my way up the path. Nearly everyone has come outside, hanging decorations and helping start the massive fire. Henry and Robert carry large plates of food and rations while Thomasin assists the younger girls in hanging their decorations from the trees. The area is lined with fresh flowers and vegetation that has just started to bloom. It truly is a magical sight, one that shall be cherished forever.

"Let me help thee," I say as I make my way to Thomasin. We hang the last bit of decorations and take a moment to absorb our surroundings.

"Oh, Emelie, 'tis truly a wonderful evening. What an incredible idea!" Thomasin says.

"Thank thee, I thought it be a fitting end to our time in these woods. The very way in which we came into our struggles, but tonight we have the chance to amend," I reply.

Thomasin smiles, turning her gaze to the others who make final preparations for the celebration. Samuel works his way outside, bringing chairs with William to surround the fire. Henry has prepared enough food to fill the table that the others brought outside, using the last of the vegetables and meat.

"For the Spring Queen!" Catherine yells in excitement. She

pulls me down to her height and places a beautiful crown of flowers on my head.

"Thank thee," I reply as I fight back tears. The site of everyone so involved and enthusiastic brings me an unexplainable amount of joy. A joy I never thought achievable after months of torture, starvation, and death.

The sun slowly creeps behind the tree line, drowning the last of light before the moon begins to rise. Our festivities are set to begin, and the weather could not be more delightful. Everyone is now outside, gathering near the growing flames before us. Intense warmth from the fire flows across my skin and the reflection illuminates across the surrounding trees. One by one the others find their place, eating food and reminiscing about days of old with their friends. Our last gathering ended in tragedy, as that night is something none of us will ever forget. But we aim to replace the memories of that horrific night with one of magic and cheer. Tonight, we honor the arrival of spring alongside our reclamation of freedom. Things will change tomorrow and perhaps it is time to address the others and await anxiously no longer.

I draw in a nervous breath, unsure of how to courageously express my words as the leader that everyone admires. Preparing a speech felt worse than truly speaking my mind, so without further hesitation, I begin. My hand goes up in the air to attract everyone's attention.

"I have a few words I would like to say," I start, "if you would all listen to me one final time. Tomorrow our lives shall change. No longer are we labeled as witches or sinners, and we have the option of returning home to reclaim our innocence. The past few months have given us starvation, torture, and death. Many of our friends are no longer with us, so this celebration is to honor their sacrifice."

Thomasin rises from her chair at my gaze, preparing to speak and reveal the memorial she has created. Proudly she picks up a sign-like object, with what appears to be carvings and words.

"I would like you all to see what we have created. We worked all day to make something in the honor of those who gave their lives since All Hallows Eve," Thomasin says as she fights back tears. She walks over and hands me the sign, indicating that she would rather have me speak of the contents.

"It is beautiful, Thomasin," I say.

The sign has imagery that the younger children have carved, such as flowers and the shining sun. But most importantly, the names of those who have passed.

"We wished to make this a night of remembrance and honor. This wonderful display gives respect to those who are no longer with us. First, our dear friend Rose courageously lost her life to this nonsense. She was a role model and friend to all of us, teaching many of us how to read and revealing the true ways of the world. Even in the end, she never lost her pride, as her final breaths were a true goodbye to us all. After her death, her home has welcomed us and allowed us to survive. May she rest in eternal peace," I say.

The others begin to show emotion and listen sympathetically to my words. While it is not easy to hear and relive such atrocities, it is a necessary step in successfully healing.

"Next is Ezekiel, and all of those who fought for our freedom and lost their lives in the courthouse. Ezekiel aimed to take care of us all, and in an act of courage he too lost his life."

Samuel looks to the ground, unnerved at the events that still haunt him deeply. Although he has made efforts and sacrificed himself to fight his guilt, he is still visibly haunted by the night in the courthouse.

"They had to confront our parents first and choose to defend our freedom with their lives rather than cower and speak false truth. For that we are truly grateful and honor their sacrifice with every passing day."

Many of the others succumbed to their injuries or did not have the will to continue while locked in the prison. I was certainly close to losing my life on those cold nights as well.

"We also lost friends to starvation, injury, and the harsh weather in the prison, and now their names will be cleared, and they shall rest in peace."

I look back down at the sign and immediately halt in my tracks. The next name on the list catches me by surprise, and I feel a wave of emotions overcoming me. Yet I must fight through the tears, as it is an honor to acknowledge those who made our survival possible.

"My brother, John, my sweet and innocent brother. He was a true joy in all our lives, and he never needed any sympathy for his ailments. John lived a life of happiness and fought for all of us with his final breath. He survived through starvation and sickness to make a false confession with the hope of giving us freedom. He watched as the other children all passed away around him. I made a promise to John that his sacrifice would be honored, and we would be free because he confessed. And now, we have a choice."

I place the sign on a chair near the fire and begin to pace a circle around the outside. The dreaded moment of my speech has finally arrived.

"Tomorrow when the sun rises, we must all make a choice.

Return to The Hollow or venture further into an unknown future. This is not something I can control or wish to decide for anyone. 'Twas an honor to guide us through this hardship. But that time has come to an end, and this is a choice that every one of us must make for ourselves. We can walk through those gates, clearing our names and returning home. Or we can pack supplies and move forward, into unknown lands and find a home like we have done here. If my judgment is of regard, then I fully support the choices each one of you shall make. You are my family, and I love you all."

I look at every face in the crowd and all further thoughts escape my mind. My only hope is that my words have honored those who have passed and that my leadership has finally concluded. "That is all I want to say."

I let out a long breath and drop to my seat. The others sit tranquil, looking at me and back at each other. I feel anxious, hiding my arm in my lap and directing my attention to the flames. My gaze remains unbroken as I wish to hide from all the eyes that have fallen upon me. It's as though the power and emotions left my body through these words, and I hope that I have played such a part efficiently. One by one the others stand, and suddenly voices begin to exclaim thanks all around me. Tears fall from my eyes at their rejoice, and they embrace each other and come to me for comfort as well. I give love and gratitude to all of those around me. Thomasin holds me in her arms, and Henry rushes to join in. Samuel comes and places a hand on my shoulder, and we all spend the next few moments taking each other's pain away and saying what feels like goodbyes. 'Tis not my place to ask my closest friends what their choices shall be, so I live in the moment and know that I will simply follow wherever they may go.

Samuel breaks free to venture over and gaze at the memorial

sign alone. He stares at the names, almost looking for answers within himself. After giving him some time, I make my way to his side with the hopes of comforting him. I feel a responsibility to provide the reassurance that he so desperately needs to hear.

"Samuel, are you truly free yourself? Do you think a life in the church is your destiny?" I ask. His only response is a nod as he fights a battle within himself. Now I place my hand on his arm and lean closer. Still, he does not break his gaze from the memorial sign of names.

"I just want thee to know, you have filled your role and can no longer blame yourself for that night in the courthouse. You took it upon yourself to risk your life and return with Gregory. I would say that is more than enough, and you deserve to make this choice like all of us. Ask yourself what it is you truly want," I say.

Thomasin notices our conversation and provides her insight as she approaches.

"Emelie, your words were truly magnificent. And Samuel, your presence was deeply missed these past few months. But look at what you have done for all of us, you stayed in that place and fought," Thomasin says. Finally, Samuel raises his eyes and scans the area. The other children dance and celebrate by the fireside. Samuel subtly smiles, looking back at Thomasin and I. Henry makes his way to our small circle and greets us as well.

"This is truly the end of our time in this forest?" Henry asks, more so to himself than any of us. "And back into that godforsaken village?"

"The other option provides much more difficulty," I state rationally, "we have little food and nearly no supplies to-"

"Yet that has not stopped us before," Thomasin interrupts,

"we have made do and turned this old home into a sanctuary. The possibilities for a better future are endless out here. Our names may be cleared, and our parents shall welcome us home, but what life will we live in The Hollow?"

"Are you saying…that you do not wish to return?" I ask.

Thomasin lets out a sigh and grabs my hand, looking at me and back to Samuel and Henry. "To put it simply, Emelie, I go where you go," she says.

Henry takes a step forward to intervene. "Aye, back home I am nothing but a servant on my father's farm. It be in my best interest to head as far as I can possibly go in the opposite direction. But, Emelie, I shall follow you with an open mind."

Both Thomasin and Henry have placed an immense amount of pressure on me to make their decision for them. It appears neither of them wish to return to The Hollow but will do so if that is where I shall go. I did not want to make such a choice, rather I wanted to follow my friends on their paths. However, the power has fallen right back into my possession.

"I see how you both wish to proceed, and I only have one final question," I reply. Immediately I turn to Samuel who has eyes on me before I can meet his gaze. "Samuel, have you made up your mind as well?" I ask.

I could never ask Samuel to leave the life he has created for himself in the village. He found a way to take our crimes and make such as positive impact out of death and torture. He stares emotionless, then slowly directs his attention to the sign one final time. His eyes read every name on the list, and then he takes a moment to look at each of us. His lips form a subtle smile at my words. The three of us desperately await his decision, but instead he takes a few steps over to the massive fire. Samuel stands just outside of the flames and slowly starts to undo his cassock. He releases the buttons and begins to remove his gown. The attire is now removed and wrapped in his hands, as he looks down and smiles at the garment. Suddenly we all gasp as he tosses the robe into the flames.

"Does that answer your question?" He asks. We all break into smiles. "And does that secure my place in hell next to Reverend Thomas?"

We laugh, embracing our friend who has now truly returned to us, and also to himself.

"So it has been settled, I will gladly follow you all into whatever awaits in our future. We shall do it together," I proclaim.

A massive relief sweeps through my veins at the realization that I will never see Warren Hollow again. This debate has burdened me ever since the night we escaped, and finally the future is true and bright. Although our situation is not ideal, we will make do as Thomasin said and support each other. I am ready to progress from everything we have gone through. Our innocence is proclaimed, and Thomas is dead. The others will safely return to the village while the few of us move forward, and that is fine by me. This brutal chapter of our lives is ending just as it began, and most importantly through remembrance of those who never held this choice.

Our small group disperses as we finally begin to celebrate the night. I make my way around the grounds, sharing what may be my final words with Robert, William, and the few others who have embarked on this tragic journey with us. Everyone remains in good spirits, slowly lowering their guard and trying to unearth the happiness that has long been buried.

We commemorate for hours on end, dancing by the flames and indulging in delicious foods. The others pass around ale and engage in ridiculous games. The weather is beautiful and the moon shines bright above the flames.

"You would have loved this," I whisper to myself in thought of my brother.

Samuel and Thomasin spend the night embracing each other and catching up on their relationship that diminished through the winter. The love that began to bloom between them was forbidden in Warren Hollow, much like any connection between us children, aside from daily duties and chores. 'Twas a sin to chase such feelings or engage in any form of adultery, but like any of us would have done, Samuel and Thomasin always found a way to spend time together. It brings me great joy knowing that what I have found in the forest, they too have found within each other.

I cannot judge the actions of Samuel and Thomasin with complete innocence, as I find myself in a similar circumstance of my own. Here I sit, finally acknowledging deeper feelings for Henry, those beyond a normal friendship. Henry confessed that he suppresses his feelings for me out of guilt and shame. And with no further denial, I may be feeling the same way as well. Perhaps it was unfair of me to finally act on such feelings while in a state of delusion, but now we are free, and I wish to properly reveal my true self to him. He still blames himself since I nearly lost my life, and for all the pain I have endured. However, I remind him constantly that I stand here today because of his bravery. He only followed my instructions, and in turn he saved my life. My only wish is that he can finally let it go and allow himself peace with the situation.

I sit lost in thought while staring for answers in the flames of the fire. My solitude is interrupted by Thomasin, who throws a rock to gain my attention. She stares at me from across the fire with a smile, needing not to say a single word to express her purpose. Stealthily she points her finger, and without even following the direction, I know it aims at Henry. He sits alone just as I, looking into the fire and perhaps sharing a similar deepness of thought. With a smile I nod my head in reply, taking a deep breath and rising to my feet.

Without any hesitation, I make my way to Henry and sit at his side. At first he seems nervous, but there is no longer any need for uncertainty. Upon starting a conversation, Henry is noticeably relieved at my initiative. Naturally we carry out the night in jest, growing closer and eliminating any despair or discomfort. As the night passes and the moon shines bright, Henry eventually uses all his courage to place his arm around me. I smile and lean into his embrace, watching the flames and engulfing myself in all that tonight has to offer. Briskly I flash a look at Thomasin, who matches my gaze with nothing but pure joy and happiness. 'Tis truly a night of magic, and only the future shall tell what is in store for all of us.

XXII

A Witch's Tale

The sound of birds on the other side of the window awakens me. I open my eyes, only to be blinded by the sun that creeps in. An anxious feeling overcomes me as I begin to gather myself. My heart feels as though it may beat out of my chest and my breathing intensifies. Trying to compose myself, I ponder why these emotions rise in my body. Perhaps I worry for my friends that wish to return to The Hollow, or the uncertainty of the future for those of us who will venture forward.

You have achieved all your desires, an escape to the forest with your dearest of friends. And most importantly, you supported each person in making their own choice. They did so at their own will and shall live by their own desires.

Maybe it is the fear of freedom that awaits me. My future is whatever I shall make of it, something I have longed for since I was younger than John. 'Tis a strange feeling, awakening on perhaps the most important day of my life. I remind myself that returning to the village, back into the custody of Mother and Father, was never truly a desire of mine. Yet we all remained close, not wanting to venture further until we knew it was the right decision. The arrival of Gregory and his good news was quite an unexpected revelation. Up until that moment, we existed as a functioning community with responsibility and duty. Everyone had a role to play, but most importantly we survived together, arguably thrived together, within the walls of Rose's home. Resources were scarce and it did not come without difficulty, but we proved that the world would not end if control was given to us. Our parents saw us as faithless troublemakers who were unfit to complete the simplest of chores. And here we are, steadily surviving after a horrendous situation. While they may never believe it, our faith has remained strong, and we often start meals or end the day with prayer. There was little mention of life back home or our time in the prison over the past few months. Perhaps there was too much pain surrounding what occurred, watching our friends die and never knowing when our time would come. The words 'witch' or 'witchcraft' have never been spoken within these walls. We are but survivors, and now the time has come to officially reclaim our innocence.

Some will do so by walking back through those gates, entering the courthouse and proclaiming their innocence in front of the very people who would have watched as a rope fastened around their neck. The rest of us will move on, continuing our journey and discovering what awaits on the path ahead. Regardless, we are now free to make the choice and free to shape the story of our lives.

I break away from my thoughts and rise to my feet. Some of the others have already awakened, likely out of similar fear and contemplation. Happily, I smile at them as I gently make my way through the home. My steps are leading me back to Rose's wonderful bochord. One last time do I wish to absorb the peace and magic of such a space. The door is open, so I enter and sit at Rose's desk. My eyes scan the walls and shelves, reflections of Rose's passion for nature and education. And once more my eyes land upon the writings that Rose began to compile herself. Of all the potions, remedies, recipes, or teachings that I have found in her home, a new book calls to me more than anything I have studied over the winter. I pull it from the highest shelf, admiring the fine leather cover in my hand. Upon opening the bindings, I discover this to be a private journal that Rose was using to document her experiences before her death.

How did I fail to notice such a writing until now?

My hand cautiously begins to skim through all the contents. In the early pages of this book, Rose was listing simple recipes and steps to aid the ill. As the work progressed, she began to use this as a journal, writing on much darker topics like witchcraft and magic. Her words indicate the crumbling of The Hollow as soon as witchcraft first became an issue. She wrote day after day, explaining how the members of the church and court came to request odd services of Rose. They asked of witch cakes, identification of Devil's marks, and visitation in dreams. Clearly these individuals held no more of an understanding of witchcraft than us children. This becomes quite clear as I continue reading her final passages.

"Nearby communities have begun trials and executions for witchcraft off of foolish accusations. It would be unwise to expect a different fate for Warren Hollow or myself. I fear we will fall fully under the rule of the church, with little intervention from the court or outsiders. Yet they all came to me for my assistance with the simplest of illnesses and issues in secrecy. These men, all of regard, visited in days of recent with daughters and wives claiming to be afflicted. There is one man behind all this growing madness, and that is Reverend Thomas."

She knew what was to come of the village, watching day after day as fear plagued reality. Members of the church and court gave up and began to follow Thomas, who graciously accepted the position. They were all confused, our parents included, and manipulated by a terrible man who had deeper intentions. We were a quiet, small, and peaceful community, unprepared for the likes of witchcraft. Even regarded court officials and clergy members did not know how to react. They were frightened, and Thomas used these occurrences to wreak havoc.

Upon turning the page and reading the final writing in Rose's journal, I truly cannot believe my eyes.

"Thomas was not the charming man I thought him to be. He deceived me and quickly revealed his true self. And now I regret our association. Our temporary paramour was a mistake, and I fear Thomas hath gone mad upon our last encounter. I informed him that I carry his child, so I hold certainty that he shall kill me to prevent such exposure. I have sworn to tell the officials of his unjust behavior, presenting all secrets to the court with hopes of banishing him from Warren Hollow as quickly as he came."

Rose's words leave me in total disbelief. Thomas and Rose had developed a forbidden relationship, and she carried his child. To hide such an immoral truth, Thomas fed off the struggles of neighboring communities, and led our small village into madness to conceal his own transgression. With Rose declining his advances and preparing to expose him, Thomas found the perfect way to silence her. This was never about any of us, or even suspicions of witchcraft. All our suffering, the death and destruction, months of losing faith and struggling to survive, was all merely to conceal the wickedness of Reverend Thomas. And then our All Hallows Eve gathering occurred, so Thomas needed to maintain such a narrative. Perhaps if we did not gather in the forest then all these events would have concluded on the day we were exiled from the church. Only Rose would have died, and that would have been the furthest that witchcraft polluted our lives. We shall never know for certain, yet I feel it justifiable to reveal such a truth to the others.

Rose lost her life to bring peace and rationality back to Warren Hollow. Before anyone could listen to her words and judge with reason, they allowed Thomas to legitimize witchcraft and used it as a medium to enact chaos. However, the very thought of confronting a witch in the prison nearly brought him to his knees.

He never believed in such a fantasy but used the struggles of surrounding communities to conceal his wickedness and get away with murder in an innocent place.

A truly unrighteous time fell upon us as a result, disrupting our lives and forever changing the future of The Hollow because of one man. It is hard to believe that those days have come to an end, and I must learn to let it go as well. Yet, after all that Rose has brought us in her life and even now, I feel an obligation to finish her story. The words spoken just before her execution burn in my mind.

"If I am to be a witch, Thomas, then you shall be the Devil here before me."

"All of our truths shall be revealed in due time."

The truth holds much tragedy. She tried to expose bearing a child, Thomas's child, and we all failed to recognize such a remark. But how could we have known? It may never be understood how they formed a relationship or what exactly occurred, but 'tis my desire to present every detail of what happened in the prison, and between Rose and Thomas, with the hope that it shall be understood. The first few chapters of this tale may have concluded, but the full story is just beginning.

For the last time I rise from Rose's desk, gathering the journal and a few other writings that will prove as useful. Out of respect I quickly organize the room, placing books back on their shelves and closing the window. I take one final look at the room, whispering a subtle "Thank you," as I close the door behind me.

The sun now shines in the sky, indicating that our time in this home has officially come to an end. Everyone is now awake and rushing around anxiously through the halls. They gather any rations they wish to take and anxiously talk of life in the village. I spot Robert and William attempting to conceal weapons within their outfits.

"Good morning to you both, I see you are returning home well prepared," I joke.

They both laugh, William pulls me in to say a subtle goodbye.

"I take it you are not returning?" William says.

"I'm afraid not, William. My calling is elsewhere, and I do not wish to return to that life," I reply.

"Very well, Robert and I both understand. We spoke to Thomasin and Samuel, who told me none but the same. Yet we feel that someone must go and watch out for the others and ensure that The Hollow is safe."

I give both Robert and William a final embrace, suspecting this shall be the last time our paths cross.

"Thank you both. We would not be here without your sacrifices and contributions. Good luck to the both of you," I say.

"No Emelie…Thank you," Robert says.

"And William," I whisper as I pull him closer, "present this journal to Gregory, it is quite important."

I hand William the journal, opening it to the last page for him to learn the truth. My trust is placed in William, as he will undoubtedly keep the journal safe. He carefully reads the words, and his immediate change of expression indicates that he understands the truth as well. He starts to raise the journal and prepares to get everyone's attention, but I pull it back down and signal for him to remain silent.

"Not now, William," I say.

"Very well, 'tis my promise that Gregory shall read this. All shall read this. The truth will be known," William replies.

I nod to William as a final goodbye, and he grips the journal tightly with both hands to signal his determination. The others shall soon know the truth, but I do not yet wish to present such findings to those of us who are not returning. Certainly I will inform them in the near future as well, but now is not the time. Thomasin, Samuel, and Henry have endured too much through this hell. To know there was no truth or justification behind it would be difficult to accept at the moment.

It fills me with joy to know that dear friends like William and Robert will watch over the other children like Catherine and Edith. And while they still have full power in deciding to head in the other direction, I understand the desire for any who wish to return home. One by one I say my final goodbyes and give thanks to the others, all of which return equal gratitude to me.

'I never wished to be a leader,' I told Thomasin, and now I hold that regard with everlasting honor. So much inner guilt and hatred. Yet I found my way, coming to peace with our experiences and learning to hold faith once more.

Truthfully, I will miss every one of my friends who choose not to join us in moving forward. Even the ones who I never spoke to until we arrived at Rose's home or in the prison. We've all endured a tragedy and somehow stand here today as survivors. We will share a lifelong bond that shall never be broken. I watch as they all gather the last of their belongings and make their way outside. Some act like me, showing an appreciation for Rose's home and getting lost in deep thought. But most of them are more than ready to move on with their lives, not taking but a single glance at their designated areas or belongings.

I am intentionally the last one left in the home. Taking one final look through each room, I ensure that the home is well kept and shall be preserved through the weather and time. Perhaps someone else will move to this home and restore life as we have done. Until then it shall sit empty, free of noise and commotion. Just like all of us, Rose's home deserves a peaceful and honest rest. I begin to feel an inner sadness, one that I have not felt since returning to my home from the prison. Some of my happiest memories with John, and Mother and Father, occurred within these very walls. Year after year I watched as Rose healed my brother and became like a sister to me. She taught me to read and opened my eyes to the world, and I shall do whatever necessary to honor her name and legacy.

Sure enough, I notice one final object that has been left behind. The memorial sign put together for all those that we have lost. I pick it up, looking at each name once more. Emotionally I pull it to my chest, holding it tightly in my arms as if they are here with me. "We made it," I whisper.

The time has finally come to exit the home. I take a last glance and pull the door closed behind me. Spring's warmth greets me as I make my way outside. Some of the others sit on the porch, while the majority stand eager to leave on the path. I look around, spotting Thomasin, Samuel, and Henry as they say their final goodbyes to the others. Rather than drawing any further attention, I casually make my way to Robert who stands eager at the front of the developing line.

"Robert," I say as I approach, "could you please fulfill one final request for me?"

Without hesitation Robert gives me his full attention and matches my tone. "Of course, Emelie. What would you like me to do?" He asks.

I raise the sign with my hand, dropping it into his arms and watching as he stares down at the names.

"Do what you must with this. Hide it somewhere for all of you to visit or put it on display near the platform of execution for everyone to see. 'Tis not of importance, just do not let anyone forget their names or their sacrifices," I plead.

"You have no need to worry, Emelie, none of us shall ever forget. And I can promise that if they wish to accept us back into their walls, then they must accept each person who is no longer with us as well," Robert says pointing towards the sign.

I smile, giving Robert one final embrace before walking to Thomasin. I make my way down the line, watching as my friends smile and prepare to return home. I understand that they all must be going through the fear and uncertainty just as I, but they have each other and that bond shall remain.

Thomasin greets me with a smile as I make my way to the smaller group. The others are prepared to leave so I feel it necessary to confirm one final time with my closest friends.

"They are all prepared to leave for The Hollow. Are the three of you certain that you wish to do this?" I ask anxiously.

"Yes," Samuel answers immediately. He appears more than eager to begin our journey and officially put this life behind him. He fulfilled his purpose, sacrificing himself and playing perhaps the most important role in ensuring everyone can return to their homes.

"I shall go provide them all with instructions and what to expect," Samuel says as he walks to the others.

"Emelie, I do not wish to be anywhere else than right by your side," Henry says as he gently grabs my hand. I smile, thankful for his presence and fully aware of my growing admiration for him. He saved my life and kept us all from starvation throughout the winter.

"On second thought…," Thomasin begins, "I simply wish to return to my mother. 'Tis not wise of me to travel with the person who nearly had me killed and labeled me the most wicked witch of all."

I laugh at her wittiness, something that never dispersed through all the hardship and torture. She is my dearest friend, a sister, and I would certainly not be alive without her. She holds me tightly, nearly taking my breath at such force.

"But perhaps I shall forgive you and come along," she says.

We both smile and engage playfully with each other, and I know the time has finally arrived. Samuel makes his way back to us as the others start on their way down the path. Gradually they pick up speed and start to race, but take a moment to turn back and begin shouting thanks and waving goodbyes. The four of us wave back and shout as they travel out of sight. It brings tears to my eyes, watching everyone rush back to their homes to reclaim the lives that were taken from them. Samuel and Gregory pulled off a miracle in restoring order to the village, and I wish everyone happiness and peace in their return. 'Tis an act of bravery returning to Warren Hollow, one that I do not believe I could perform myself. Yet the younger children do not understand, and some of us simply wish to return to the way things were. It may never fully be the same as it was, but an attempt is being made on all sides. The witch hunt has reached its end, and we can finally live our lives once more.

The others are out of sight and the four of us stand in silence. I take a moment to smile at Samuel, Henry, and Thomasin, showing gratitude for their presence. We are finally on our own and have endless possibilities. Perhaps we shall travel far across the continent, stopping to meet others and experiencing all that the world has to offer. Maybe we will find a larger home, one grand enough to house all four of us. Or maybe we shall discover another village that will accept us and allow for a new beginning. We all sit and ponder these choices until Thomasin disrupts the silence.

"Now what?" she asks.

We all laugh at such a ridiculous question, and more so at the ridiculous situation we are now in. The four of us are nothing but young adults, prepared with minimal supplies and completely on our own. 'Tis a fearful but exciting feeling.

"I know of a place," Henry says as he steps forward. "My family raised me on a farm that was far away from here. It was a massive home, surrounded by lands of forest and vegetation. We were forced to leave because Father nearly burned the farm down during one of his drinking fits. My Uncle Nicholas and Aunt Amelia lived there with us, and I am certain they could still be there," Henry explains.

"How far away is it, Henry? And you remember the way?" I ask.

"Yes, we left when I was quite young, but I will remember. From here it may be a one-month journey, maybe two or three given our lack of transportation. It sat near a village like The Hollow, full of wonderful people. A thriving community that simply grew tired of my Father. But I know for certain they would welcome us. I could assist with the farming and you three could easily make something of yourselves as well," Henry claims excitedly.

"Sounds good to me," Thomasin says in agreement.

Samuel also looks at Henry and nods in approval, and then all three of them turn to me. It certainly sounds like a swell idea, reaching a place where we would be welcomed with a fresh start. Somewhere far away, a wonderful farm with a thriving community nearby. The journey shall not be easy and knowing it may take months is a challenge. We do not have a wagon, or even a single horse, but together we will endure, and I would follow my friends anywhere that they desire.

"Perhaps we should be on our way if we wish to arrive before the winter comes once more," I reply.

Henry smiles and we all share excitement at such an adventure. We gather our rucksacks of supplies and prepare to begin our expedition. And for the final time, I say goodbye before we embark. Not to Rose's home, Warren Hollow, or my friends, but to myself. The person who often escaped to solidarity in nature, who was an accused witch, who lost a brother and countless friends, who sat helpless in a prison cell wishing to die, who nearly met death on more than one occasion, who was beaten beyond recognition and lost a hand, who committed murder, who was a leader, and who somehow survived every second of it. I am at peace with myself and wish to leave all this hardship behind. These experiences shall never be forgotten, but it is time to start anew and become more than what Reverend Thomas made me. My life is now in my control, and I have my friends to help me endure.

Without further hesitation we are on our way, heading in the opposite direction of Warren Hollow and the lives we are putting to rest. I cannot help but take one final glance over my shoulder at Rose's home as it falls out of sight.

About the Author

Ajay Bell makes his writing debut with <u>Watch Over Me: *A Witch's Tale*</u>. Born and raised in Pittsburgh, Pennsylvania, Ajay graduated from La Roche University in 2022. Holding a lifelong passion for the horror genre, alongside the gained knowledge and respect for literature through his education, Ajay found inspiration and decided to become a first-time author. Ajay presents a unique writing style, honoring the darker side of literature with an articulate focus on the grim and gothic nature of the world. When Ajay is not obsessing over all-things horror, he can be found practicing martial arts.

www.ingramcontent.com/pod-product-compliance
Lightning Source LLC
Chambersburg PA
CBHW050311110726
47899CB00007B/2201